**"Even now you know the truth, it makes no difference."**

"I agree," James drawled. "And not telling me the truth wouldn't have, either. I would have known the moment I made love to you."

"James, haven't you heard a word I've said? I can't be involved with you."

"Loving me isn't being involved?" he mocked.

Aura sighed. "I will not expose you to the lies the press will print about me if they find out we love each other."

"It wouldn't bother me in the slightest," he said dismissively. "But if it bothers you, we'll have a quiet wedding."

"Wedding!" she spluttered. "I'm not going to marry you!"

"Of course you are."

**CAROLE MORTIMER**, one of our most popular—and prolific—English authors, began writing in the Harlequin Presents series in 1979. She now has more than forty top-selling romances to her credit and shows no signs whatever of running out of plot ideas. She writes strong traditional romances with a distinctly modern appeal, and her winning way with characters and romantic plot twists has earned her an enthusiastic audience worldwide.

## Books by Carole Mortimer

Don't miss any of our special offers. Write to us at the following address for information on our newest releases.

Harlequin Reader Service
901 Fuhrmann Blvd., P.O. Box 1397, Buffalo, NY 14240
Canadian address: P.O. Box 603,
Fort Erie, Ont. L2A 5X3

# CAROLE MORTIMER

## secret passion

*Harlequin Books*

TORONTO • NEW YORK • LONDON
AMSTERDAM • PARIS • SYDNEY • HAMBURG
STOCKHOLM • ATHENS • TOKYO • MILAN

For John,
Matthew and Joshua

Harlequin Presents first edition April 1988
ISBN 0-373-11069-3

Original hardcover edition published in 1987
by Mills & Boon Limited

# CHAPTER ONE

THE man seated behind the imposing desk was not the one Aura had come here to see, and the light of battle began to fade from her eyes.

She turned sharply to the secretary who had been about to show her into the office. 'I think there has been some sort of mistake——'

'No mistake, Miss Jones.' The man behind the desk stood up as he spoke, and Aura immediately understood the reason for the dark, solid furniture in the room; this man would have looked ridiculous against any other background.

He was very tall, well over six feet, with a lithe body not usually seen on a man who worked behind a desk all day, the superbly tailored suit he wore emphasising his lean masculinity. Just to look at him was to get a feeling of power, of barely leashed strength.

Aura took in his appearance in a matter of seconds, even acknowledged that he had an attraction that was as powerful as his body: thick dark hair neatly styled to his ears and collar, its slight inclination to curl ruthlessly kept in check, brilliant green eyes that looked her over speculatively as she stood poised in the doorway, his mouth a sensual slash beneath an arrogantly jutting nose, his jaw square and firm.

But it wasn't what he looked like that concerned

her, but who he was!

'Thank you, Moira.' He smoothly dismissed his secretary as he strode across the room to close the door behind Aura. 'Please, sit down,' he invited softly.

She had come prepared to do battle, and instead she had been greeted by a complete stranger. Where was Adrian? She looked about her awkwardly.

'Please,' the man prompted again, his eyes narrowed at her apparent reluctance to stay now that she was here.

Aura sat down in the chair that he had indicated facing his desk, wishing she had thought to telephone to make an appointment before rushing over here. But she had been so angry ...!

Her mouth tightened as she remembered the reason for her anger, sherry-brown eyes sparkling warningly. 'I came here to see——'

'Mr Mayhew,' the man finished as he moved softly around the desk to resume his seat.

*Mr* Mayhew? She hadn't called Adrian anything that formal for weeks!

'I'm afraid he isn't here at the moment,' the man excused lightly. 'And as you said, the matter you need to discuss was of some importance ... My name is Ballantine, Miss Jones,' he added briskly as she still looked uncertain. 'Mr Mayhew and I are business partners.'

Her eyes widened. James Ballantine; he wasn't at all what she had expected Adrian's partner to look like!

Adrian gave the impression that he worked with a

much older man, and yet Aura was sure this man couldn't be much older than his mid-thirties, possibly a little younger, which would make him only four or five years Adrian's senior. Adrian spoke of the other man as if he were Methuselah!

Her mouth tightened as she remembered her reason for being here, and the fact that Adrian couldn't be relied upon to be completely honest about anything, let alone admit that his partner was really a powerfully attractive man.

'I really would prefer to see Mr Mayhew,' she bit out tautly.

Dark brows rose over speculative green eyes, deep slashes of displeasure grooved into his lean cheeks as his mouth firmed. 'I believe I just told you my partner isn't available at this time.' His voice had hardened too. 'I can assure you, Miss Jones, that anything you wished to say to Mr Mayhew you can now say to me.' Those grooves in his cheeks disappeared as his mood relented a little, although his impatience was barely concealed behind the polite façade.

Aura gave an inward sigh. She certainly couldn't say *any* of the things to this man she had intended saying to Adrian!

But there was still the problem of the letter; *that* wouldn't go away, no matter which of the partners she talked to.

She looked closely at the man facing her; had Adrian told his partner about her, had they laughed together as Adrian made one of those man-to-man jokes about her? James Ballantine returned her gaze steadily enough, but that didn't mean he wasn't completely aware of Adrian's 'personal' interest in her the last few weeks.

But what choice did she have, it was either talk to this man or no one. And there was always the possibility that she had misjudged Adrian. Although she didn't think she had.

She opened her clutch-bag to take out the official-looking envelope. 'I received this this morning.' She thrust the unfolded letter across the desk at James Ballantine, normally tranquil brown eyes snapping with anger.

Long lean fingers took the letter from her grasp, while the other hand lifted black-rimmed glasses that had rested on the desk top, to place them high on the bridge of his nose. He briefly scanned the letter, his brows raised questioningly as he once again looked up at her. 'This seems very straightforward.' He placed the letter down on his desk, regarding her through the slightly tinted lenses of his glasses.

She was well aware of the 'straightforwardness' of the letter, knew the exact wording on the single sheet of paper without needing to read it again. The lawyers who acted for Ballantine and Mayhew had written to inform her that the lease that ran out on her shop next month would not be open for renewal, and could she please have the premises vacated by the given date!

The letter had been waiting for her just inside the door of the shop this morning, and after making a few telephone calls she had left her assistant in charge while she went to see Adrian. The last thing she had expected was that Adrian would be out and that she would have to deal with his partner instead. Did this man have any idea of the vindictiveness behind the letter? He wasn't a man who revealed his thoughts easily, and the glasses acted as another shield to his emotions.

'The wording of the letter *is* very clear,' she acknowledged tightly.

He frowned at the admission. 'Then what appears to be the problem?'

'The *problem*, Mr Ballantine,' she bit out tautly, 'is that when I signed the initial lease two years ago it was with the understanding that it would be renewable at the end of that time.'

'Subject to both parties' approval.' He nodded slowly.

'Yes. But——'

'Obviously, from this letter, you can see that we don't approve,' he reasoned impatiently, obviously wondering why she was wasting his time over something that was already so clear.

Gold sparks flashed among the sherry-brown of her eyes, the below-shoulder length of her pale blonde hair seeming to crackle with anger. 'Why has my lease been singled out for refusal of renewal?' she rasped. 'I've checked with your other tenants at Cooper Mews, and all of them have renewed their lease in the last twelve months.' Telephone calls to the neighbouring shops were the only reason she hadn't been here earlier this morning, needing to be sure of her facts before confronting Adrian.

James Ballantine raised dark brows. '*You've*

checked?' he repeated mildly.

Aura wasn't fooled by that mildness for a minute, knew that, despite his politeness to her so far, the lines of hardness around his eyes and mouth indicated he could be a very dangerous man to cross.

'Of course I checked,' she confirmed impatiently. 'We aren't just talking about my livelihood here, I also happen to live in the flat above the shop.'

'Alone?'

He seemed as surprised by the question as she did, his gaze suddenly challenging.

Surely if Adrian had told the other man about his involvement with her James Ballantine wouldn't have needed to ask such a question, Aura reasoned.

'No,' she bit out, not enlarging on the statement, deciding that if Adrian hadn't already told this man about her, her living arrangements were none of his business; her lease didn't say anything about listing the occupants of the flat above the shop.

'I see.' His tight-lipped disapproval was tangible as he picked up the letter to read it once again. 'Have there been any problems with payment on your part to precipitate this move by us?' he murmured frowningly.

'Certainly not!' Her eyes flashed her indignation.

He shrugged, throwing the letter down on top of the other papers littering his desk. 'Then perhaps there has been a mistake made by our legal department,' he said thoughtfully. 'I don't believe we have any other plans for any of the properties we own at Cooper Mews.'

Aura was *sure* they didn't, was equally sure that

Adrian was behind this move to deprive her of her shop and her home. The old saying warned 'beware of a woman scorned'; no one seemed to consider that it was a warning that should also apply to a *man* scorned. One man anyway.

James Ballantine looked at the rapidly changing expressions on her face with piercing eyes. 'If you would just leave this matter with me——'

'I've always dealt with Mr Mayhew in the past.' It was because of a contractual problem concerning the roof that she had first met Adrian, having received no help from the legal department here. After that first meeting Adrian had made a point of calling round to the shop from time to time to make sure things were running smoothly. Then a few weeks ago those visits had ceased to concern the shop ...

'I can assure you, Miss Jones, that I am quite capable of dealing with this matter myself,' James Ballantine informed her glacially. 'If you would just leave this with me I will get back to you.'

She knew he was furious at her persistence, but her shop was just one of hundreds of properties the partnership of Ballantine and Mayhew owned. 'When?' she demanded abruptly.

He drew in a ragged breath, as if he weren't accustomed to having his movements questioned. And maybe he wasn't, but Aura couldn't afford to have him put the problem of her lease—and her—to one side, and just forget about them.

In the almost two years since she had opened 'Health is Wealth' she had built up a steady clientele, adding new customers to their number all the time as more and more people became aware of healthy food as a way of *being* healthy.

The shop had become her salvation, occupying her time and thoughts completely, and she wasn't about to lose it because a man she had stupidly considered charming had found that he couldn't control his libido!

After weeks of casual visits from Adrian to the shop the flowers had begun to arrive. Daily. Until Aura had broken all her own rules and agreed to have dinner with the sort of charmingly wealthy rogue she had sworn never to be involved with again.

That first dinner together had been followed by yet another, and then another, until she realised she had been seeing him at least a couple of times a week. He was pleasant company, attractive enough in a rakish fashion, and if his goodnight kisses at her door could become a little too demanding on occasion, he never made any effort to get beyond the door. A week ago she had realised that was all part of his strategy, a strategy he had soon tired of when her curiosity hadn't become piqued and *she* had been the one to do the inviting.

Her twenty-fourth birthday had loomed bright and clear, and she had been thrilled with the lovely red roses that arrived for her from Adrian, less than pleased with the diamond bracelet he presented to her over dinner that evening. Her refusal to accept such a gift from a man she considered a friend had resulted in the rakishly attractive man becoming viciously nasty as he informed her he had no interest in being her '*friend*', that he wanted to be her lover. And soon.

She had cursed herself, and him, on her taxi-ride home, for not seeing sooner that he had deliberately lulled her into a false sense of security before revealing what he really wanted from her.

His retaliation to her rejection of him as a lover had arrived in the letter she had received from the lawyers of Ballantine and Mayhew today, she was sure of it. Just as she was sure that if she agreed to let Adrian into her bed after all, the matter would instantly be dropped.

Maybe it was lucky after all that Adrian wasn't here at the moment and she was dealing with James Ballantine; his involvement could be her only way out of this situation. Even if this man knew of her past friendship with his partner, she couldn't believe he would approve of Adrian's harassment of her. She needed this man on her side.

'Miss Jones,' he began slowly in answer to her terse demand. 'Our acquaintance has been a short one, but I was not aware that I had done anything during that time to make you doubt my ability to carry out the simple task of checking the contents of this letter with my legal department.'

Aura flushed at his unmistaskable sarcasm. Maybe she was being unfair to him, but after Adrian's underhand methods of persuasion, who could blame her!

'I'm sorry,' she muttered awkwardly. 'I'm just—a little anxious.'

His expression softened slightly, although his

mouth remained forbidding. 'I can understand that,' he soothed. 'And I really will get back to you as soon as I know anything.'

It was a dismissal, she knew that, and after her forceful behaviour she couldn't really blame him for wanting to get rid of her as soon as possible. 'I am sorry.' She looked at him appealingly, her eyes warm, her full mouth curved stiffly above her pointed chin, the freckles that covered her nose and cheeks more noticeable against her pallor, due to the tension she was under. 'But to you it's just another piece of property, whereas to me——'

'I *do* understand, Miss Jones, and I—excuse me,' he rasped impatiently as the intercom buzzed on his desk. 'Yes, Moira?' He spoke tersely, all the time looking at Aura, as if her tenacity were a little beyond him.

'Your luncheon appointment is here, Mr Ballantine,' he was informed.

'I'll only be a few moments longer,' he told his secretary before turning his full attention back to Aura. 'I have to go,' he said abruptly, taking off his glasses to dazzle her with deep green orbs while he placed the glasses in his breast pocket.

Prudence warred with necessity as she considered meekly accepting this second dismissal in as many minutes—and the latter won! 'You won't forget about my lease during your—lunch-break?'

Anger flared in the dark green eyes, to be replaced by incredulity—and finally humour. 'Miss Jones——' he glanced down at the letter on his desk. 'Aura,' he amended. 'You are without doubt the most outspoken young lady I have ever met.'

She winced. 'I am?'

'You are,' he drawled, smiling slightly, this time the grooves in his cheeks not looking at all menacing, 'I am on my way to a business luncheon, not my mistress's bed!'

A delicate blush coloured her cheeks. 'I'm sure I didn't imply——'

'Yes, you did,' he mused. 'And I suppose I should be flattered,' he added drily.

She didn't know why. He was undoubtedly a sensual man, despite that rather unapproachable air he wore like a protective cloak; a man didn't reach his mid-thirties without realising his sexuality was a tangible thing, no matter how well he tried to subdue it. 'I just assumed——'

'Too much,' he put in softly. 'I don't have a mistress, Aura. Or a girlfriend. Or even a casual date.'

She couldn't tear her gaze away from his, sherry-brown locked with emerald green. Why had he told her *that*, for goodness' sake? He surely didn't think that she——! 'Your personal life—or lack of it—holds no interest for me, Mr Ballantine,' she snapped coldly. 'It's your business interests that concern me.'

He gave a weary sigh, rubbing his temples with long sensitive fingers as his elbows rested on the desk-top. 'The day started out so well, too . . .'

Her mouth tightened. 'I'm sorry if I've done anything to ruin that for you——'

'No, you aren't,' he derided. 'You had something to say, and you would have said it no matter who you upset.'

'Yes,' she grimaced.

He laughed softly, his eyes warm, the amusement remaining in his smile. 'I'm not upset, Aura,' he murmured thoughtfully. 'Intrigued, perhaps, but certainly not upset.'

She stood up abruptly; the last thing she needed was a complication like this man in her life! 'I've taken up enough of your time.' She moved determinedly towards the door.

Somehow he was there before her, having crossed the room with a stealthy grace that was unnerving at the same time as his suddenly close proximity sent a shiver of awareness down her spine.

'You haven't taken anything I wasn't willing to give,' he told her softly.

Aura looked up at him with alarm, that alarm increasing at the unmistakable warmth in sensual green eyes. 'I have to go,' she insisted sharply.

He nodded slowly. 'I'll be in touch.'

Now what did he mean by that, she puzzled irritably all the way down in the lift and on the walk out to her car. The last thing, positively the *last* thing she needed, was for Adrian's partner to become interested in her.

Unless the two men *had* discussed her, she worried on the drive back to the shop. James Ballantine didn't seem the type of man to indulge in locker-room gossip, but that didn't mean Adrian hadn't told him about the obstinate woman he was dating who refused every move he made to share her bed. Maybe he had even challenged his partner to see if he could do any better with her!

She wouldn't put that sort of challenge past the type of man Adrian had proved himself to be, but she was sure James Ballantine wasn't like that. She was letting her insecurities of the past colour her judgement.

But no matter what conclusions she came to about James Ballantine, it didn't alter the fact that Adrian had repaid her rejection of him by refusing to renew her lease, or that once Adrian returned to the office later today he might manage to convince his partner that he had acted that way for a good reason, and James Ballantine might just decide to go along with that decision . . .

It wasn't the most relaxing day she had ever spent, expecting a furious Adrian Mayhew to appear in the shop at any moment, at the very least anticipating a telephone call from James Ballantine to tell her there was nothing he could do about renewing her lease.

Neither of those things happened. Each ring of the bell over the door as it opened brought in only customers, and the only two telephone calls she received were from other customers with queries. By five-thirty, as she and Jeanne, the middle-aged lady who helped her run the shop, closed up for the day, Aura's nerves were frayed to breaking-point.

'Everything all right?' Jeanne took time out from the mad dash she always had at the end of her working day to get home and cook the dinner for her invalid husband and their three young children. 'You seem very tense,' she explained her concern.

Aura sighed. 'It's just been one of those days,' she

evaded; the other woman and her husband had enough trouble meeting their bills as it was, without worrying them with the fact that Jeanne might soon be out of a job because the shop was having to close. 'I'm sure it will be better tomorrow.' Oh God, she hoped so. If James Ballantine didn't call her first thing tomorrow morning she was going to call him, and damn the fact that that was sure to make him angry straight away!

Once Jeanne had left to hurry to the nearby supermarket before it closed she paused while cashing up to look around the shop that had become her pride and joy. It was light and airy, the shelves well stocked and varied. It was *hers*, damn it, and she refused to lose it because Adrian didn't like to hear the word no! She would take him to court over it if necessary—no, she wouldn't do that, she admitted to herself dully. She wouldn't do anything that would draw attention to herself, and claiming sexual harassment by her landlord would certainly do that!

But all the anger and frustration of her situation faded as soon as she looked at the gentle face of the woman waiting upstairs for her in the flat. No one, least of all she, was able to resist this delicately lovely woman's vulnerability, Aura feeling protective as soon as she looked at the other woman.

'Hello, Mummy.' She greeted her mother softly so as not to startle her.

Vague brown eyes focused on her with effort as her mother looked up from the television set showing a popular children's cartoon. 'Is it that time already, dear?' She frowned as she saw the till-roll and books in Aura's hands.

'Yes,' she confirmed indulgently, kissing her mother on the cheek before glancing at the television screen. 'Has the cat been put out for the night yet?' she mused.

'No, dear.' Her mother patted her cheek. 'And talking of cats, have you seen Marmaduke today?'

'He came in with me and went straight for his food bowl in the kitchen,' Aura assured her, knowing how her mother fretted about the wandering tomcat. 'Just give me five minutes and I'll get our dinner started.'

'I'll get it, shall I, dear?' her mother offered, but her attention had already wandered back to the television programme.

Aura smiled as she went up to the next floor to her bedroom, knowing her mother would still be immersed in the cartoon—or another programme like it—when she went through the lounge in a few minutes on her way to the kitchen. Every night her mother offered to get dinner for them, and every night she either forgot or wandered off to do something else.

At only forty-five, with the sort of beauty that had only increased with the years, her mother had retreated into a world where pain didn't touch her, where she saw only good in everything, because to see things any other way would be to see reality. It had been like this since Aura's father died.

Her mother had never been a forceful personality, but the death of the man she loved had somehow pushed her into a world where she took responsibility for nothing, and where no one expected her to do so. When she wasn't watching the childishly uncomplicated programmes on television she would just sit and daydream, and from the faraway tranquility of her expression when she did that Aura guessed her thoughts were as childishly unfettered by reality.

Shock, the doctors had diagnosed her condition, at the sudden death of Aura's father. They had all predicted she would as quickly recover from the shock, that it was something that occasioanlly happened to the deeply grief-stricken. They had been wrong, and despite constant counselling, her mother still lived in that state where she knew the man she loved had gone, but where she preferred to think he had just briefly left their lives.

At times Aura felt her father's loss so acutely she wanted to share her own pain with her mother, but as time passed and her mother continued to live in her world without pain the doctors had feared that the sudden jolt into awareness could result in permanent damage. Sometimes, as Aura watched her dreamily vague mother, she wondered if it weren't already too late to do anything to help her.

Once she had changed into peach cotton trousers and a brown blouse, she went down to the kitchen, her mother, as she had predicted, still watching the television, having switched off the news in favour of a nature programme.

Aura didn't know how her mother would react to the move if they had to make one. She didn't seem aware of her surroundings most of the time, had made no comment when they moved here two years ago, and yet this flat was part of her mother's security.

Her mother's distracted, 'I could have done it, dear,' as they sat down to the dinner Aura had prepared, made her smile sadly.

Her mother had never been a forceful person, had always been content to go along with the will of the majority rather than argue her own point of view, but Aura *did* remember her as a woman whose complete happiness enveloped all around her; the way she was now, neither happiness nor despair touched her. It was heartbreaking for Aura to witness.

The fact that Adrian, when he had called for her here, had been unfailingly kind to her mother had only made her like him more; now she was sure that kindness had just been another part of his plan to persuade her into a deeper relationship with him.

Her sudden loss of appetite was due solely to Adrian Mayhew and what he was trying to do to her, and she refused her mother's offer of helping her clear away, needing to be alone to try to work out what she would do if James Ballantine refused to reconsider renewing her lease. She would have to look for another property if that happened, and she wearily thought of the time it would take to find somewhere that was suitable. Why didn't—who was her mother talking to? Oh God, she hadn't started talking to herself too, had she!

Aura was hastily wiping her hands dry as she rushed into the lounge, entering the room just in time to see her mother inviting James Ballantine into the flat.

He looked over the top of her mother's head at her flushed and dishevelled appearance, frowning at her suddenly fierce glare. 'If I've called at an inconvenient time ...?'

Any time would be inconvenient with him looking like *that*!

He ought to have a 'Danger' warning sewn onto the waistband of the faded denims he wore; the way they clung to his hips and thighs was positively indecent. He had no right to reveal how broad his chest was in the dark green shirt and black leather jacket, and he certainly had no right to have his hair falling rakishly over his forehead like that, ruffled by the gentle breeze outside!

Aura realised she had stopped breathing as soon as she saw him only because her starved lungs suddenly demanded air, her ragged breath audible as her mother moved to turn down the volume on the television set.

'Not at all—Mr Ballantine, wasn't it?' Her mother gave him one of her vague smiles. 'Aura has just finished clearing away. And I——'

'Mummy,' she warned as her mother picked up a book that lay open on the sofa.

'—was just off to my room,' she finished serenely as if Aura hadn't spoken, dazzling James Balantine with another of her beautiful smiles before going up the stairs.

James Ballantine watched her go with vaguely disturbed eyes. 'She's very lovely,' he said suddenly.

'Yes,' Aura snapped, suddenly in control again. OK, so out of the dark suit he had worn earlier today and wearing casual denims and a leather jacket instead, he looked devastating; that was no reason to forget that this man had to be here for a purpose, and she had to know what that purpose was. 'Have you come to tell me——'

'She seems a little—not quite of this world.' He still gazed after her mother.

'Yes,' she bit out tautly. 'Now would you——'

'But so very beautiful,' he said again dazedly, as if completely mesmerised.

'Mr Ballantine——'

'James,' he corrected gruffly, crossing the room to her side in two strides. 'Don't expect me to be coherent when I've just seen what you're going to look like in twenty years' time,' he murmured softly. 'Aura . . .!'

She didn't have time to prevent the contact as his head bent to hers and the mouth that she had classed as sensual on sight took possession of her. That was the only way to describe what happened to her, James not just claiming her mouth but branding the whole of her body with his touch.

One hand curved about her nape while the other one held her tightly about the hips, making her aware of the difference in their heights as the hardness of his thighs was crushed against her stomach, stirring a strange emotion there while the hand at her nape offered her mouth up to his like a sacrifice. Like a starving man he took and took, and still he hadn't taken his fill. Not that Aura didn't take too, standing on bare tip-toes to entangle her hands in the thickness of his hair as she matched the hunger.

She looked up at him with dazed eyes as he slowly put her back down on the carpeted floor, wondering how she had ever thought him unapproachable, his emotions held firmly in check; there was no mistaking the hunger displayed in his eyes—and it was all directed towards her!

She stepped back, swallowing hard. 'You shouldn't have done that.' She should have sounded firmer and not quite so breathless! He *shouldn't* have done that, had left her weak and dazed.

'I'm going to do it again in a moment,' he promised throatily. 'But before I do we had better get business out of the way; I don't think either of us will be capable of discussing it later on!' he added ruefully.

She held up protesting hands. 'What happened between us——'

'Happens every time I look at you,' he admitted softly, dark green eyes devouring her parted lips as his gaze rested upon them. 'I want you.'

Aura was speechless. Men just didn't *say* things like that, so bluntly it made her blush. They flattered, and cajoled, and coerced, they didn't *tempt*. And that last description fitted exactly what James was doing to her, only having to look at *him* to feel a leap of her senses. But the first three exactly described what Adrian had *tried* to do to her.

Her mouth tightened at the thought of the other man. 'You said you came here to discuss business,' she prompted abruptly.

'To start with,' he drawled, reaching into the inside breast pocket of his jacket to hand her the envelope he had removed. 'Your lease,' he explained at her questioning look. 'All it needs is your signature, duly witnessed, of course.'

Aura gaped at him, sure she couldn't have heard him correctly, quickly opening the envelope to stare at the legal document. It was the lease to her shop, for the length of five years. It was more than she had hoped for. More . . .?

Her smile faded as she looked up at James warily. 'What's the price?' she snapped.

He frowned. 'The terms are in the agreement——'

'I meant *your* price.' She looked at him challengingly.

He became suddenly still, and if she had thought him unapproachable this morning she now knew what unapproachable was! His eyes were glacial, his mouth a thin angry line, those ominous slashes grooved into his cheeks. And Aura knew with certainty that she had completely misunderstood this man's motives in helping her.

'I'm sorry,' she rushed into breathless speech. 'I just—why did you—and your partner, change your minds?' she frowned.

'We didn't,' he rasped. '*I* had never refused to renew your lease, and Adrian obviously only made the mistake in his haste to be off on his holiday. I'm sorry you've had to be upset in this way, but that's the only explanation I can give you for the mistake.'

She had really insulted him, and he wasn't going to forgive her easily. But she had been so used to dealing with men like Adrian! 'I really am sorry I thought—that, about you, James. I——'

He visibly relaxed. 'I'll forgive you—because you called me James for the first time.'

He had far from forgiven the slight, she could see that, but he was willing to forget it, for the moment. 'I—if your partner is away, and unable to sign this document,' she began slowly, chewing on her inner lip, 'is it still legal? And binding?'

James smiled at her suspicion this time. 'Completely,' he drawled.

'But——'

'"Oh ye of little faith",' James mocked. 'One of these days you'll have to tell me why you're so distrusting. But not now,' he accepted ruefully at her silence. 'OK,' he sighed. 'Well, whenever either my partner or I are away the other has complete power. My God, if I had to wait for Adrian's approval to anything every time he took his wife on holiday I'd never get anything done!' he scorned.

Aura felt herself pale. *Wife?* Adrian was *married?* Oh God, not again, she *couldn't* go through that again!

# CHAPTER TWO

'He,' James continued gratingly, unaware of Aura's distress, 'takes Selina away with sickening regularity.'

She swallowed hard. Married. Why hadn't she realised that? 'Sickening?' she echoed dully, lost in the misery of what could have happened if she had been attracted to Adrian enough to accept the intimate relationship he had wanted.

'Mm,' James sighed his impatience. 'You would have to know Adrian well to realise why. My business partner isn't—well, he isn't as faithful as he could be. Damn it, he isn't faithful at all,' he rasped disgustedly. 'As soon as his latest affair ends he whisks his wife away on an expensive holiday. I think his guilty conscience catches up with him,' he added grimly.

Latest affair? Oh God, was that *her*? Well, unless Adrian had met someone in the last week it had to be! She felt *ill*. 'Doesn't his wife realise what's going on?'

James turned away. 'I've never spoken to her about it,' he bit out.

A wife could usually tell if it went on long enough, and if Adrian made a habit of this ...! 'Perhaps she doesn't mind,' Aura suggested lightly. 'Some women don't, you know.'

He shrugged. 'I really wouldn't know, Selina

doesn't discuss her marriage with me. But after ten years of it——'

'He's been unfaithful to her all that time?' Aura gasped.

His mouth twisted. 'I would say that even Adrian was faithful to begin with. Besides, there was Robert to consider.'

Aura blinked, almost afraid to ask the question, but knowing she had to. 'Robert?'

'Their son,' James confirmed her worst dread. 'He's nine now, and away at boarding school most of the time, but I'm sure my partner would have been a little more discreet in his actions when the boy was still at home.'

A child was involved too. It was like a sickening re-run of a nightmare. Adrian had acted nothing like a man with a wife and child to go home to, hadn't seemed to care what time of night he left her, or how often he came to see her and took her out. Surely his wife *had* to realise there was something strange about his constant absences? Maybe she considered the holidays ample recompense. She knew of other women like that.

But what she had learnt about Adrian today made Aura want to run away and hide so that no one need ever know that she had been out with him. My God, when she considered the times she had been out with him; anyone could have seen them together. She wouldn't be able to survive another scandal like that.

She looked at James Ballantine with wary eyes. 'I shouldn't keep you any longer. Thank you for bringing round the lease, and——'

'Aura,' he cut in gently, 'when I told you earlier today I don't have a mistress, a girlfriend, or a casual date, I should also have included a wife to that list.' He put his arms about her. 'I'm not a married man.'

She was relieved to learn that, but she still couldn't have anything to do with this man. If he should ever realise that *she* had been his partner's 'latest affair' . . . Well, not quite, but who would believe a denial of that coming from her? And she was sure that when this man looked at a person with disgust they would feel as if they had been *burnt*.

She tried to pull out of his arms. 'I think you should go——'

'I'd rather not,' he groaned into her hair.

She stod completely still. 'I'm *asking* you to go,' she said shakily.

He drew back slightly to look down at her. 'Aura, I realise we don't know each other very well——'

'We don't know each other at all,' she corrected—and as far as she was concerned it was going to remain that way!

James smiled at her stubborn expression. 'That can easily be remedied——'

'I don't want to know about you,' she told him vehemently.

'—I'm thirty-four,' he continued as if she hadn't interrupted. 'The only son of deceased parents. I like children, and animals—especially cats,' he added as the sleek ginger tomcat entered the room. 'Hello, boy,' he greeted, going down on his haunches to tickle the ecstatic animal behind the ears.

'Marmaduke,' Aura supplied abruptly. 'He belongs to my mother.'

'He's a beauty.' Piercing green eyes suddenly looked up at her. 'Couldn't we have dinner together one evening?'

She drew in a sharp breath at the abrupt change of subject, sure he had deliberately tried to catch her off guard. 'No,' she answered firmly.

He straightened, ignoring the ginger cat as it twined in and out of his legs at the sudden, deprivation of his caressing fingers. 'You have—someone, in your life?' His eyes were narrowed.

If she said yes, would he go away and leave her alone? The determined set of his mouth said no, that he would merely set about eliminating the competition. 'Is it unusual for a woman to say no to you, Mr Ballantine?' She was deliberately scoffing.

'One that kisses me the way you do, yes,' he nodded slowly.

A flush burnt her cheeks, and she knew this man wasn't flirting with her, that he didn't know the meaning of the word; he seduced with candour and the certainty of his own feelings. 'Mr Ballantine, I have no wish to have dinner with you,' she told him abruptly. 'I have a business to run, my mother to take care of——'

'That can't take up all your time,' he chided.

'It does!'

'What do you do for relaxation?'

She sighed. 'I read, occasionally go for long walks, play tennis——'

'I'll pick you up Sunday afternoon and we'll hire a court for a game——'

'—badly,' she finished ruefully. 'Martina Nav-
ratilova has nothing to fear from me.'

'Sunday,' he said again firmly. 'Two o'clock. I'll
give you a coaching lesson; John McEnroe taught me
everything I know about tennis.'

Her eyes widened. 'You know——? But——'

'I'll see you Sunday afternoon, Aura.' He gave her
a quick kiss on her parted lips before leaving.

For seconds after he had gone Aura was unable to
move, unable to believe she actually had a date with
James Ballantine despite all her objections. He was
attractive and sensitive, but he was also one of the
most forceful men she had ever met!

She moved to the curtained window, drawing one
of them back just in time to see the sweeping U-turn
of a sleek grey Jaguar as James accelerated the car
away.

She had a feeling that when James wanted
something badly enough, as he had seemed to want
her company on Sunday, he just refused to accept the
word no. As Adrian had? No, she was sure that James
would always deal fairly for what he wanted, that he
always attained it without hurting anyone to do it.
Hadn't he just done so? She wasn't hurt; she was
bewildered and slightly off-balance, but she wasn't
hurt.

'Has Mr Ballantine gone, dear?' Her mother
sounded disappointed as she entered the room from
the stairway.

'Yes.' Aura was still a little dazed.

'Such a nice young man,' her mother smiled
warmly, having an ageless quality about her that

refused to recognise she was only a few years James Ballantine's senior. 'Will we be seeing him again, do you think?' she asked innocently.

'No. Yes. No! I don't think so,' Aura said with determination.

'What a pity.' Her mother sighed. 'He had such kind eyes.'

Aura looked indulgently at her mother, a woman who saw no evil in anyone or anything. Although she had, Aura recalled with a frown, remarked upon the fact that Marmaduke didn't seem to like Adrian, and that 'animals knew, didn't they?' At that time she hadn't paid too much attention to the vaguely made comment, but now she looked at her mother with sharp query.

'You deliberately made sure I couldn't talk to you until today, didn't you?' Aura glared accusingly at James as he drove the Jaguar with relaxed control.

It was Sunday, and promptly at two o'clock, as she had known he would, James had arrived at her home. He had then proceeded to charm her mother with gentle teasing, and enlist her help in persuading Aura to take a break when she had already told him she didn't have the time to play tennis—no matter who his personal coach had been! He had even asked her mother if she would like to join them, genuinely disappointed when she had politely refused.

He glanced at Aura now with innocently wide eyes. 'I don't——'

'And don't deny it,' she warned. 'I've been calling your office for the last two days, and each time your

secretary told me you were "unavailable",' she said
with disgust.

'And you don't believe I was?' he mused softly.

'I'm sure you weren't,' she snapped impatiently.

'I'm a very busy man, Aura,' he mocked.

'Not that busy!' she glared.

He sighed. 'You're right. I told Moira not to put
any of your calls through to me so that you couldn't
cancel our date for today.'

'It was *your* date, I don't remember at any time
agreeing to it. And you might at least have lied about
your duplicity,' she added disgustedly.

He looked at her intensely. 'I'll never lie to you
about anything, Aura.' His hand covered hers as it
rested against her thigh, the brief white shorts she
wore leaving most of her long legs bare. 'I want you
to always remember that.'

The cool touch of his fingers against her skin, the
knuckles brushing her thigh as he briefly clasped her
hand, had completely disarmed her.

She had no idea what she was doing here with him,
had intended sending him away as soon as he arrived
today, and instead, at his and her mother's insis-
tence, she had meekly found herself changing into
the shorts and a brief white sun-top.

Maybe it had been the way that he looked in his
own white shorts and T-shirt that had thrown her;
she had taken one look at him as he stood on the
doorstep, his legs tanned and muscled, his arms and
torso rippling with power, and she hadn't been able
to say no to joining him for a game of tennis. What
could possibly be wrong with a harmless game of

tennis? she had told herself as she changed. Looking at him now she knew exactly what was wrong with it; she wouldn't be able to concentrate on anything but the complete masculinity of this man. She had a handicap before they even started the match, and there was no such thing as a handicap in tennis!

'You *could* always have asked Moira to pass on a message,' James said softly at her silence.

Aura looked at him, and then quickly looked away again. She *could* have asked his secretary to give him a message. Why hadn't she? She couldn't actually have wanted to spend the afternoon with him; it would be pure madness to allow herself to be attracted to him. She was *already* attracted to him; the madness would be to do anything about it!

'I didn't think of it,' she told him abruptly.

He looked disappointed that she wasn't about to give him the same honesty he had promised her. 'Did you know that when you lie the freckles stand out on your nose?' he confided softly.

Her hand automatically moved up to cover her nose and those tell-tale freckles. 'James——'

'I wish your mother had agreed to come with us,' he remarked thoughtfully, cutting off her protest. 'She's very pale, I think the fresh air might have done her some good.'

Aura turned away, her hand dropping back to her thigh. 'She doesn't go out much.'

'What happened?' he frowned.

'Trauma,' she supplied abruptly. 'My father's death,' she added at his expectant silence.

'I'm sorry,' he told her gently. 'It must have been

awful for both of you.'

'Yes,' she acknowledged abruptly. 'She likes you,' she heard herself add, and then wondered why she had done it; the last thing this man needed was another dose of self-confidence, he was already arrogant enough for two men, had completely taken her over since they had first met. She had gone to the offices of Ballantine and Mayhew to do battle, and instead ended up with this forceful man in her life. 'I'm not altogether sure she's a good judge of character,' she told him caustically.

He smiled. 'Of course she is.' He sobered. 'Can anything be done to help her?'

'Not unless you can bring my father back.' She couldn't keep the edge out of her voice. 'Unless you can do that I don't think she wants to be helped.' She turned her attention to their surroundings as she sensed his sharp gaze on her. 'Are we almost there?'

'Almost,' he confirmed distractedly. 'Aura——'

'Do you really know John McEnroe?' she asked sceptically.

He looked as if her disbelief had deeply offended him. 'Of course I know him.'

Five minutes into their game of tennis Aura knew that whatever his coach had *tried* to teach James about the game, very little of it had actually been absorbed or utilised.

She eyed him mockingly after winning the first set six love. 'OK,' she sighed. 'So who was he?'

'Who was who?' James was busy wiping the perspiration from his brow, having been running all over the court chasing the ball.

Aura felt a little sticky, but she hadn't even worked up a sweat, sitting beside him on the wooden seat at the side of the court. 'The John McEnroe you know,' she said drily, sure it hadn't been *the* John McEnroe.

'He was my sportsmaster at school,' James revealed unabashedly, his hair damp across his forehead. 'I believe his opinion of my game was that I "showed absolutely no aptitude" for it.'

Her mouth twisted. 'I can believe that. I've never won a set from anyone before, let alone whitewashed them!'

His eyes were warm as he gazed up at her, his arms resting along the length of his thighs as he sat forward. 'My talents obviously lie in other directions,' he told her softly.

Aura readjusted the colourful band about her forehead. 'How did you and your partner ever go into business together when you seem to have so little in common?' She deliberately opted for an innocent channel for his 'talents' to be directed in.

He shrugged broad shoulders, the T-shirt clinging damply to his back. 'His father was initially my partner, and when he died I inherited Adrian,' he added drily. 'It has, to say the least, been a rocky partnership.'

She wished now that she hadn't introduced the subject of Adrian into the conversation; just talking about him made her remember what a fool she had been about him. 'Do you want to play another set or would you like to go and get an ice-cream? My treat,' she offered.

'The ice-cream can wait.' He stood up fluidly. 'I

have to try and leave this game with a little of my dignity left intact.'

He was definitely an athletic man, obviously kept himself fit, and yet when it came to tennis he just didn't have the co-ordination. It was nice to know there was something he didn't do well!

She took pity on him in the second set and let him win one game, although she still won the match six-love, six-one.

'I think I've suffered enough humiliation for one day,' he said with a grimace, putting away their rackets. 'A work-out in the gym and jogging are my usual forms of exercise.'

She had guessed he hadn't attained that physique just sitting behind a desk all day, had found it hard not to let her attention sway to the masculine power of his body as he moved around the court rather than concentrating on the game. And she had no intention of falling a victim to that power again.

'Come on,' she teased. 'I know a place where they serve ice-cream that's home-made and hasn't been crammed with a load of additives.'

The shop was run by a friend of hers, and the two of them strolled into the park opposite as they ate them.

'You're really into healthy food yourself, aren't you,' James remarked admiringly.

She nodded. 'I have a friend who has a little boy who becomes a monster when he eats any food that contains the additives E100 to E300. When he was younger she fed him on all the things it's easy for little children to eat, hamburgers, sausages, white bread, cakes, crisps—interspersed with the goodness of vegetables and fresh fruit—and he was like something demented most of the time. Helen, his mother, nearly had a nervous breakdown because he was so bad. He was aggressive, violent, didn't sleep at night—and so neither did she. It became so bad that Helen finally insisted their doctor refer him to a psychiatrist.'

'And?'

'And apart from the fact that he was hyperactive they said there was nothing wrong with him,' Aura drawled. 'And so it went on, with Helen becoming more and more run down, and Jonathan being a little demon. And then one day Helen read an article on colourings and preservatives in food, and the effect they could sometimes have on children. She was so desperate by this time that she would have tried anything. She changed his diet completely, which didn't please him at first, especially when he had to drink pure fruit juice instead of the diluted or fizzy kind—most of *them* are full of colourings and flavours. Within three days Jonathan was already a different child, bright, happy, *loving*. It was difficult to believe the difference it had made in him. At first Helen feared it might just be a fluke, that any day he would revert to the little monster. It's been two and a half years now, and he's one of the most adorable children you could ever wish to meet—as long as he doesn't accidentally get any of those additives in his food! Helen has even had a second child, something she swore she would never do after the first year she had with Jonathan.'

'Where do you come into it?' James asked, interested.

'At the time people were still very sceptical about the harm of the additives, especially as they make the food look and taste more attractive most of the time, and a lot of the manufacturers refused to accept that their products could produce this Jekyll and Hyde effect. Consequently Helen had tremendous difficulty finding food for Jonathan that wouldn't make him feel too different from everyone else. I was looking for a business at the time——'

'So you opened "Health is Wealth",' James realised appreciatively.

She nodded. 'I'm sure that if those additives can be harmful to children then they must also be harmful to adults, in ways we don't even realise. I refuse to have anything that contains additives in my shop. You have to eat healthily to be healthy, I believe. Does that sound too much like preaching?' she grimaced, realising how long she had gone on about her favourite subject.

He shook his head. 'It sounds like a woman who believes in something.'

She gave a rueful shake of her head. 'Like a woman who had Jonathan to stay with her for a week to give Helen a break—*before* she had managed to sort out his diet,' she corrected self-derisively. 'After only one day with him I understood why Helen couldn't cope. As for the nights——! Five minutes' nap in between hours of playtime nearly killed me. Of course some children just are hyperactive, although luckily Jonathan wasn't one of those ones. He often stays with us now, he and Mummy get on very well together.' Because Jonathan accepted 'Aunt Meg' exactly as she was.

'I don't know what was in or out of it, but the ice-cream was delicious.' James put the last of it in his mouth before throwing the tub in the bin.

Aura was suddenly mesmerised by the smear of ice-cream on his top lip. What would his reaction be if she reached up and——

His eyes darkened. 'Lick it off, Aura,' he encouraged throatily.

Her breath lodged in her throat, her startled gaze clashing with his, a blush darkening her cheeks as she realised he had been well aware of the eroticism of her thoughts. 'We had better be going——'

'Not yet.' He clasped her shoulders, his hands a sensual caress against their nakedness. 'Lick it off, Aura,' he urged again. 'I want to feel your tongue on me.'

Aura didn't think her breathing would ever return to normal as it once again stopped in her throat. He wanted to *feel*——! The images that statement aroused in her mind went much further than his top lip.

'Please, Aura!'

His eyes compelled her to move, and she slowly went up on tip-toes to place her mouth against his.

As always, when she was close to this man, she was lost at the first touch, their mouths open and moist as they tasted each other.

James finally raised his head. 'Your tongue, Aura,' he groaned raggedly. 'Give it to me!'

Her eyes closed as he enfolded her against him, feeling dizzy and excessively warm at the same time, obeying his command mindlessly, tasting him and the ice-cream together, having no doubt about which one was making her head spin; she had eaten a whole tub of the delicious ice-cream without feeling in the least light-headed, but the smallest taste of James left her hungering for more.

And she took more, moving down his jaw and throat with open-mouth kisses, reaching the open neck of his T-shirt, the slightly salty taste of his flesh making her thirst, and melt, and *ache* . . . !

His hands threaded through the silky softness of her hair as he raised her face to his once again, the kiss fiercer this time, their bodies touching from chest to thigh.

Aura felt herself spinning out of control, wanting to be even closer to him, caressing the hardness of his back as she clung to him.

'—youngsters of today have no shame,' muttered a disgusted male voice. 'In our day we would at least have gone somewhere a little more private to do that sort of thing!'

It took a few seconds for the words to penetrate the sensual spell Aura and James were under, but it finally did, and they looked about them dazedly, the park as deserted as it had been earlier—except for an elderly couple walking their dog some distance away, the woman seeming to be asking her husband exactly how often he had 'gone somewhere a little more private to do that sort of thing' when he was younger—because he certainly hadn't been with *her* at the time!

Aura and James looked at the elderly couple and then at each other, their joined laughter breaking the sudden tension.

'For my part,' James drawled drily, 'I'm just grateful to be included under the term "youngster"!'

'I think I am too,' Aura laughed softly as they walked side by side back to the car. 'Anyone over twenty-one is considered old nowadays.'

'In that case I'm ancient—and being with you makes me feel far from that.' He unlocked the car door for her. 'I've enjoyed today,' he told her softly as he got in the car beside her, making no effort to turn on the ignition.

She swallowed hard. 'I have too.'

'Can we do it again?'

'Me slaughter you at tennis?' She attempted to tease, her palms damp with tension. How could she not see him again when she enjoyed being with him so much! He made her laugh, was genuinely interested in what she had to say, made her feel very much alive and aware of what was happening about her. She hadn't felt so alive since—she couldn't *care* for this man, she realised desperately. 'I don't think so,' she told him harshly. 'It wouldn't be a good idea to mix business and—and pleasure.'

'You have enjoyed being with me, then?' His eyes were narrowed, those ominous grooves in his cheeks appearing and disappearing, as if he couldn't decide if he were angry or not.

'Who doesn't enjoy winning?' She deliberately

misunderstood him.

His mouth tightened, the grooves very much in evidence now. 'There isn't going to be a loser between us, Aura. We can both win, if you'll only let us.'

'I really do have to get back now,' she told him lightly. 'I don't like to leave my mother alone for too long.'

'The subject of my taking you out again is closed?' he rasped.

'Yes.'

'Very well.' He nodded abruptly, switching on the ignition. 'But I'm not going to lose you now I've found you.'

Why did that sound so much like a promise, and not a threat?

# CHAPTER THREE

THE next day he came to the shop to buy everything he needed for a 'naturally healthy diet'; the day after that he came in to tell her how much healthier he felt already and to deliver some magazines he had thought her mother might enjoy reading; the day after that he arrived with an article he had found on additives that he thought might interest her.

He was pushy in the nicest possible way, possibly because he knew she wouldn't accept anything else; she was sure he wasn't usually quite this obliging, always making sure he never stayed long enough that she had to ask him to leave. It was as if he were making a place in her life for himself without making her feel any pressure, and she knew she was coming to look forward to his daily visits in spite of her dire warnings to herself that she shouldn't.

'Is James coming over this evening, dear?' her mother asked eagerly over their early dinner.

Aura had been waiting all day for him to turn up at the shop, intending to tell him that the visits had to stop. When he hadn't arrived she had been disappointed instead of relieved, and that made her angry. 'I have no idea,' she dismissed tautly. 'But if he does I won't be here!'

Her mother blinked at her vehemence. 'Has he done something to offend you?'

Only become a necessary part of her life. And she

wouldn't, she *couldn't* accept him into it. James might not be a married man, but there was too much danger attached to going out with him, and it didn't just come from her innocent involvement with Adrian.

'No,' she assured her mother lightly, rewarded by her mother's serene expression. 'I just told Helen that I would go over to see her tonight, Simon's away on business and she could do with a little company.'

'That will be nice,' her mother approved. 'I often think you don't get out enough. Especially now that Adrian——'

'Whatever you do don't ever mention Adrian to James,' she said frantically as she realised her mother was one way James *could* find out she had once dated his married partner, albeit unknowingly.

'As if I would, Aura,' her mother reproved gently. 'James seems to be a very possessive man to me; I doubt he would like to hear about the men you saw before the two of you met.'

She frowned. 'Mummy, I hope you aren't reading more into James's visits to us than is actually there?'

Her mother gave one of her more serene smiles. 'Of course I'm not, dear.'

Now why didn't she *feel* reassured by that assurance? Possibly because her mother had shown a decided preference for James from the first, and because his kindness to her mother was something he genuinely felt and not just something he affected for her benefit. Between the two of them she could find herself involved in a situation that could only spell disaster!

'Leave that,' her mother suggested as Aura stood

up to clear away. 'I can do it.'

She was about to refuse the offer, sure the dishes would still be sitting there when she came down from changing, but then she remembered the doctor's instructions about letting her mother take on responsibility if she asked to do so. Maybe they *would* still be there when she came back downstairs, but she would never know if she didn't let her mother try.

'Thanks, Mummy.' She kissed her warmly on her smooth cheek. 'I'd like to try to get to Helen's before Jonathan and Annie go to bed.'

'Give the little darlings a hug from me,' her mother said.

To Aura's surprise the table had been cleared when she returned a few minutes later, and from the noises she could hear coming from the kitchen the dishes were being washed too. She couldn't remember the last time her mother had carried out even so simple a task.

With sudden clarity she knew that it was James's influence that had achieved this. Her mother hadn't shown this much liking for any man since Aura's father died, and although Aura was sure there was nothing in the least romantic in her mother's feelings towards James, she also recognised that her mother was flowering under his marked attention. That complication could make it impossible for her to ask James to stay out of their lives. God knew she wanted her mother back as she used to be!

Her mother was in the process of putting things away when she joined her in the kitchen, the tears that had blinded Aura's vision minutes earlier in the lounge as she envisaged a life of normality with her mother firmly held in check.

'That's a nice outfit.' Her mother stopped to compliment her. 'Are you sure you're only visiting Helen?' she teased.

A blush darkened her cheeks as she knew she was a little overdressed in the burgundy blouse and matching trousers to visit her friend and her two boisterous children, but if there was a chance of James coming here tonight she wasn't about to let him see her looking a mess. 'I'm sure,' she chided lightly. 'I shouldn't be too late,' she added in parting.

She wasn't sure but she thought she heard her mother say, 'I'm sure we'll manage to amuse ourselves,' as she closed the door!

Did her mother *know* James was coming here tonight, she paused in the lounge to wonder. Probably not for certain, but after his non-appearance today it was probably a good guess.

'Going on somewhere?' Helen greeted her after opening the door to her knock.

'Very funny,' she scowled, following her friend through to the lounge, at once feeling soothed by the absolute chaos that ensued when a three-and-a-half-year-old and a one-year-old got together, toys all over the carpeted floor, the two dark-haired children in their midst arguing about the possession of a bear that didn't look as if it was going to survive the clash.

Their cries of 'Aunt Aura!', 'Ant Awa' settled the argument, the bear completely forgotten as the two sturdy children stampeded across the room to launch themselves into her arms, the two tiny bodies smelling of talcum powder and soap where they had been bathed and dressed in their matching Snoopy pyjamas ready for going to bed.

'Have you been good for your Mummy while Daddy's away?' she asked sternly.

'Yes,' Jonathan answered her earnestly, used to the game.

'Oh yes.' Annie caught on very fast, an ebony-haired, blue-eyed smaller version of her brother and mother, their father Simon having blond good looks.

'For tomorrow.' She held out the two chewy bars she knew they could both eat without having a reaction to it. 'When Mummy says so,' she added gently.

'Right, you two,' Helen cut in indulgently. 'Now that you've seen Aunty Aura it's time for bed——'

'Oh but——'

'I'll come and help Mummy tuck you both in,' Aura promised, Jonathan happily accepting the compromise as he put his hand in hers, whereas once he would have thrown himself on the floor in a temper tantrum for not getting his own way.

Bedtime for these two adorable children was always a special time to Aura, and she sat in Jonathan's room with his mother as she read him a good-night story, Annie already in her cot, fast asleep by the lack of noise coming from the room next door.

'So.' Helen eyed Aura speculatively, the two children asleep, the lounge returned to normal, both of them sitting down for a welcome rest. 'What's been happening to you lately?'

She shrugged. 'We've been very busy at the shop. And the——'

'I meant personally,' Helen drawled, a few years

older than Aura, the two of them having been friends
from childhood, their homes quite close to each other
then. 'Your mother said you were out with James
when I had a chat on the telephone with her Sunday.'

'Oh,' she sighed, relaxing back in her seat. 'Well,
I'm not seeing him any more.'

'Why not?'

'Oh, Helen, you know why not,' she chided
impatiently. 'I don't get involved with men, especially men like James. If I didn't know it before, my
disastrous relationship with Adrian more than
confirmed my belief that men like that just aren't for
me. James is a prominent businessman too, obviously
comes from a wealthy background——'

'That's no guarantee that he knows the Sutcliffes,'
Helen put in softly. 'Adrian didn't seem to.'

She drew in a ragged breath. 'That's no guarantee
that James doesn't. The fact that he's wealthy has to
increase the chances that he might. I can just see it
now, the two of us out for a nice cosy dinner for two
and one of his friends comes along and recognises me.
As well as being devastatingly handsome he's a good
man, a completely honest one.' Very honest, she
remembered ruefully. 'He wouldn't understand.'

'Then tell him the truth,' her friend said simply.

Her eyes widened, as startled as a fawn's when
confronted with danger. 'You mean——' She swallowed hard. 'You mean——'

'I mean that you should tell him the truth before
he hears that nonsense version of what happened,'
Helen said calmly.

'I couldn't.' She shook her head, her hair loose

about her shoulders. 'I—he isn't that important to me.'

'Isn't he?' Her friend looked at her closely. 'Then why do you look as if you aren't sleeping, and just the mention of his name puts you on edge?'

'I—look, I hoped you would help cheer me up,' she said briskly. 'Not lecture me about a man I just met!'

'I'm not lecturing,' Helen sighed. 'I just don't like to see you wasting your life.'

'It isn't wasted,' she protested. 'I enjoy my life just as it is.'

'Do you?'

'Yes!'

Her friend sighed. 'Uncluttered by men,' she drawled. 'Simon can be a pest at times, but I wouldn't be without him.'

She felt a wistful ache in her chest for the love she knew existed between Helen and Simon, and for a brief moment indulged in the fantasy that such closeness could one day be hers, perhaps with a man like James. But it *was* only a fantasy, the reality was that he was more out of reach to her, because of his wealth and position, than most men were.

'Are you taking my name in vain?' teased a mocking voice.

Helen's face glowed with happiness as she jumped up to rush across the room into her husband's waiting arms. 'You said you couldn't get back until tomorrow,' she chided between kisses.

'I thought I'd surprise you,' Simon grinned down at her, his arm about her shoulders as he turned to look at Aura. 'Is that sexy outfit just for Jonathan's benefit?' he teased.

'No, I hoped you would be home tonight,' she returned seductively, this light-hearted flirting having become a habit between them from the moment they had first met, all of them aware that there could never be another woman for Simon but Helen.

'Just let me get rid of my wife——'

'Simon Collister!' he was warned threateningly.

He laughed softly, a tall leanly built man with laughing blue eyes and an unruly thatch of blond hair. 'This is the life, *two* beautiful women waiting for me to get home.'

'One,' Aura corrected, standing up to kiss him on the cheek. 'I'm going to leave you two to go upstairs and look at the children and then say hello properly.'

Simon sobered, frowning slightly. 'That isn't necessary——'

'It is necessary,' she insisted firmly. 'I know that if I——'

'Yes?' Helen prompted softly as she broke off abruptly, a dark blush to her cheeks.

'If I had a husband as handsome as Simon I'd want to be alone with him after being separated for three days—and nights,' she teasingly added, knowing by the sceptical rise of her friend's brows that Helen wasn't fooled for a minute. Aura trembled as she realised what she had been about to say.

What *would* it be like to have a man like James come home to her every night? The evocative thought haunted her on the drive home. Would they share the open warmth and love that Helen and Simon had? She didn't doubt that James would make a wonderful husband, that once he had made a commitment to a woman he would remain faithful to her the rest of his life, would love her exclusively. Only Aura knew she could never be that woman.

Finding him at her home, engaged in a game of Scrabble with her mother, wasn't conducive to her peace of mind!

The two of them were seated on the sofa, the board in front of them on the coffee-table, and from the empty coffee cups and long list of the scores on the pad beside James he had been here for some time.

He looked up at her as she paused in the doorway, his eyes warmly appraising behind the tinted lenses of his glasses.

After the thoughts Aura had been having about him his smile was almost her undoing. Then she forced herself to remember how dangerous it was to be attracted to this man. Allowing her guard to drop with Adrian had almost been her undoing, and James would demand much more from her than a physical relationship; he was a man who would want it all.

She looked at him coolly, remaining aloof even when he frowned. 'Enjoying your game?' she greeted him lightly, entering the room.

'Oh my.' Her mother looked at the clock on the mantel. 'Is it that late already? Did you see Marmaduke on your way in, dear?'

'He's probably out with his latest girlfriend,' Aura dismissed drily. 'Don't go, Mummy,' she said sharply as her mother stood up. 'Stay and entertain your guest. It's been a long day, I think I'll go to bed.'

'Darling, James is *your* guest,' her mother chided. 'He was just kind enough to play a game with me while he waited for you to come home.'

Gold glittered in sherry-brown eyes as she watched as her mother said goodnight before going up to her bedroom.

She turned on James as he slowly put his glasses in the breast pocket of his jacket as it lay across the arm of a chair. 'I thought I told you I didn't want to see you again,' she attacked.

He nodded, the overhead lighting making his hair appear ebony. 'And I told you I wasn't giving up,' he reminded her softly.

'There's nothing to "give up"——'

'You want me too, you know damn well you do,' he rasped, frowning darkly.

'And do you think I take every man that I want to my bed?' she scorned. 'Do you have every woman you decide *you* want?'

'There really haven't been that many,' he said, his eyes narrowed.

'I can't believe that,' she scoffed. 'You're thirty-four, unmarried, very eligible; of course there have been women.'

'There *have* been women——'

'I know that,' she scorned.

'Aura, I refuse to be baited into the argument you're spoiling for,' he bit out, his mouth tight, those ominous grooves etched into his cheeks.

Her face was flushed as he guessed what she was trying to do. 'Because I refuse to be a number to you,' she told him heatedly.

'Damn you, stop this!' He shook her roughly. 'You're different, Aura——'

'Aren't we all?' she mocked recklessly. 'Variety is the spice of life, and all that——' James's mouth came punishingly down on hers, cutting off further speech. 'No!' She wrenched away from him, tears glistening in her eyes. 'I won't be used!' She glared at him.

His hands fell away from her shoulders. 'I don't want to use you, I want to love you,' he groaned, his expression pained.

'Until the next woman you want to *love* comes along,' she scorned.

'Someone once hurt you very badly, didn't they?' he rasped impatiently. 'Do you think that gives you the monopoly on pain and disillusionment?' he challenged. 'I can assure you it doesn't! I found out my fiancée was cheating on me only a week before we were to have been married. *Yes*, there have been women since that time,' he confirmed harshly. 'Half a dozen at the most. And none of them wanted more from the relationship than I did!'

Aura was speechless. James had once cared enough about a woman to want to marry her. Why did that knowledge cause her such pain?

'Do you still love her?' she frowned, all the fight gone out of her.

He shrugged. 'I'm not sure what I felt for her. I was your age at the time, saw her through the innocent eyes of a first love—until I found out that my treating her with respect bored her out of her mind and that she had turned to someone else to give her the excitement our relationship lacked. I've never offered another woman that respect.'

Aura swallowed hard, knowing he had offered it to her—and she had thrown it back in his face. 'I'm sorry. I shouldn't have pried.' She pushed her hair back from her face. 'I was feeling bitchy, and I—I hit out at you.'

'Because I'm trying to get too close,' he acknowledged, his eyes narrowed.

'Because you won't go away and leave me alone,' she nodded abruptly.

'If you don't feel anything towards me, why should it matter so much?' he reasoned.

'You don't understand.' She shook her head. 'It isn't a question of how you make me feel,' she sighed. 'I don't want to become involved with you. I like my life as it is——'

'You like shunning affection from other people because that way you can't be hurt again? You like being alone even when you're with other people? You actually *like* living on that island of emotions where nothing can touch you?' he rasped harshly.

The tears welled up and splashed over, wetting her cheeks. He *knew*, this man really knew what it was like to exist in that sort of solitude, to feel the pain of loneliness deep inside you where it never went away!

'It doesn't have to be like that, Aura,' he groaned, his arms going about her shaking body. 'God, I'm not asking you to give up that protection to take a chance on me. All I want is that you try, Aura, try to give a little at a time. I won't ask for more than you want to give.'

He had already taken so much from her, his own disillusionment with the past making him understand her too well, able to knock down the protective walls about her heart with his persistence. 'There's nothing for me to give you.'

'There's that warm, beautiful woman inside you,'

he corrected. 'The woman who cares for a mother a lot of people would have become impatient with and placed in a home.'

'My mother isn't insane,' she flared defensively. 'She's just—different.'

He nodded. 'That doesn't alter the fact that a lot of children in the same circumstances would have had her locked away,' he said grimly. 'I want the woman who loves her mother enough not to do that. Also the woman who cares enough about her friends to help them when things get rough—not many would have taken on a child like Jonathan for a week the way you did.'

'They would for a friend like Helen,' she insisted vehemently. 'When everyone else——'

'Yes?' James prompted softly as she broke off abruptly.

'Helen stood by me at a time when I desperately needed—a friend,' she evaded tautly. 'I couldn't do any less for her.'

'Because that's the sort of woman you are,' he nodded. 'The sort of woman I want.'

'Why me?' she cried. 'There must be hundreds of women out there with the same qualifications.'

'Not in quite the same combination. Besides,' he added teasingly, 'I've become addicted to your freckles.'

'James——'

'Oh, Aura, *this* is why it has to be you,' he told her throatily as his head lowered and his mouth moved against hers.

She gave a choked cry, leaning weakly against him, wanting to push him away, but needing his strength at that moment. *This*, the blinding sensual pleasure they found in each other's arms, had been right between them from the beginning, and she needed him too much to fight it.

'Aura!' He trembled violently against her at her surrender. 'Oh *God*, Aura!' He drew her fiercely against him.

He nibbled, he sipped, he *drank* from her parted lips, crushing her body against his, pushing them both to the point of madness.

Aura knew her blouse had been pulled free from the waistband of her trousers as she felt James's hand sear her naked flesh, his fingers splayed across her back, moving in a sensual rhythm.

Her head was thrown back as that hand closed possessively over her breast beneath her lace camisole, her fiery gaze meeting his openly hungry one, watching the emotions flickering across his flushed face as he caressed her, her breath catching in her throat as his thumb brushed across her nipple.

'Look at me,' he pleaded as her head dropped against his chest. 'See what touching you does to me!'

Her blouse was unbuttoned, her camisole raised, her uptilting breasts bared invitingly, the nipples deeply pink from his caresses. It was agony to see the sensual torment on James's face.

'Watch,' he instructed gruffly as he bent his head and lightly sucked one pouting nipple into the moist pleasure of his mouth, moving back slightly to trace the hardness with the tip of his tongue.

Aura was lost in the spell of the eroticism, mesmerised by the darkness of his cheek against her creamy flesh, the sucking movement of his lips and tongue drawing her fully into his mouth, filling her body with a fiery warmth, feeling a moistness between her thighs, aching there.

She cradled his head against her now, increasing the pressure, wanting more, wanting—

'Touch me, Aura,' James anticipated her need, guiding her hand down on to him, instantly feeling the leap of his desire.

She wanted him. In that moment she wanted him to the point of madness, could taste him, felt the imprint of his body against hers, and she wanted so much more, sobbing her need.

She was going to explode in a moment, going to shatter into a million pieces. She needed, oh God she needed——

'No more.' James moved sharply away from her as she twisted against him, groaning as he saw the pain of rejection in her eyes. 'Darling, if I made love to you now—and God knows I want to!—you would never forgive me. A little at a time,' he reminded her soothingly. 'We'll give each other a little at a time. And then maybe eventually we'll be able to give it all.' He gently straightened her camisole and rebuttoned her blouse, smoothing her tangled hair.

Aura looked at him dazedly. He could have made love to her, could have taken the one thing most other men were interested in. Instead he had said no for both of them, hadn't rejected her but had taken the control she had momentarily lost.

This man was too much, too gentle, for her to say no to!

And that frightened her.

'James, I——'

'What was that?' he asked sharply, turning to listen.

Aura frowned. 'I didn't hear anything.' She shook her head.

A puzzled frown marred his brow, and then he shrugged, relaxing slightly. 'Maybe I was mistaken—no,' he rasped, releasing her to turn away. 'I did hear something.' He strode across the room to the door, wrenching it open. 'What the—oh no,' he groaned, bending down on one knee, his head bent.

A feeling of panic assailed Aura. 'What is it?' she rushed forward.

James turned to stop her before she reached his side. 'Please don't——'

'Oh, my God!' She stared in horror at the bundle of orange fur that lay at his feet, the once glossy coat now matted with dirt and blood, lots of blood. 'Marmaduke!' she groaned weakly.

# CHAPTER FOUR

'I DON'T think you should try to move him.' James held her back as she would have picked up the injured cat.

Her hand froze in mid-air, her gaze fixed on the cat that had been with them ever since he was a kitten. 'Is he still alive?' Her voice was hushed.

'Barely,' James revealed grimly. 'What little strength he had left seems to have been used to drag himself up here. He looks as if he was hit by a car. Do you have the telephone number of your vet?' he frowned.

She couldn't take her eyes off the tiny bundle of fur, so still now when he had been into mischief from the moment he came into their home at nine weeks old, the smoothness of his tummy barely moving as he breathed. 'It's in the book next to the telephone under V,' she answered James distractedly. 'I can't believe my holding him would hurt him any more than when he crawled up here to us,' she looked up at James appealingly. It just didn't seem right not to give her old friend the comfort of her loving touch.

James looked undecided for a moment and then he nodded. 'I know I don't have to tell you to be careful with him; you're infinitely gentle with those you care about.'

Marmaduke gave a little cry as Aura gently picked

him up, his eyes flickering open, licking her arms as he saw who his rescuer was. The tears streamed down Aura's cheeks as she sat with him cradled on her lap, just letting him lie there, not attempting to touch him in any other way in case she caused him more pain. He seemed to be very badly cut, and James was probably right about the cause being a car; the traffic could be very heavy in this area. Marmaduke had lived in a more rural area for the first four years of his life, had ruled his territory with iron paws, and he hadn't adjusted well to his change in environment.

It was all her fault. If she hadn't moved them——

'He's coming right over.' James ended his call to the vet. 'How's Marmaduke?' He came down on his haunches beside them.

'In pain,' she choked, flinching as the cat gave another low cry.

'Hey,' James chided, touching her tear-wet cheeks. 'Cats have nine lives, remember?'

'He's used up more than that since we came to live here,' she groaned. 'He didn't see many cars before that, and now he just seems to think they're large cats that he doesn't want intruding on his territory.'

'I——'

'Is there anything wrong, Aura?' her mother called down the stairs. 'I heard James leave, and then I heard voices down here again. Are you—Marmaduke?' She had reached the foot of the stairs, crossing the room, looking more fragile than ever in the pale blue nightgown and robe she wore.

She frowned at her mother's pained expression. 'Mummy——'

'Is he—is he———?' Her mother's face had drained of all colour as she saw the cat's unnaturally still body and the blood matting the fur. 'Oh my God, he's———'

'No, Mummy, he———' Before Aura could reassure her any further her mother had sunk to the floor in a dead faint.

She closed her eyes as the world seemed to close in about her, opening them just in time to see James lifting her mother from the floor and placing her carefully on the sofa. 'Marmaduke was a gift to my mother from my father,' she revealed dully.

'I see,' James grimaced, looking down at the pale-faced woman.

Aura could see that he *did* see. 'If anything happens to him . . .'

James looked at her sharply. 'You don't think she'll survive it?'

'No,' she choked. 'Silly as it sounds, I don't think she could.'

'It doesn't sound silly at all,' he assured her grimly. 'We'll just have to make sure the cat lives!'

If sheer will-power alone could do it then Marmaduke wouldn't dare leave them, James telling the cat over and over until the vet arrived to examine him that he had to live because too many people loved him, leaving the cat's side only once, and that to soothe her mother as she regained consciousness. Once the vet arrived James didn't relinquish control, instructing the man to do everything in his power to save the cat. When Aura's mother became too distraught by the examination he helped her up the stairs to her room and put her to bed, assuring her he would let her know the news as soon as they knew anything.

The examination revealed several severe cuts and loss of blood, but there appeared to be no broken bones, and no internal injuries. Aura thought she was going to faint when the vet anaesthetised Marmaduke and began to stitch up the wounds, James insisting the cat couldn't be moved to the surgery as the other man wanted him to be, assuring him that he couldn't get better care there than he would at home.

Once the cat had been cleaned up and stitched up and put in his basket to sleep off the pain and the effects of the anaesthetic Aura went up to see her mother while James showed the vet out.

Wide brown eyes looked at her in panic as her mother sat stiffly in the bed. 'Is he——?'

'He's fine,' Aura quickly soothed, briefly outlining the injuries, not wanting to frighten her mother more than she already was. 'The vet says there's a fifty-fifty chance,' she finished reluctantly.

'Is James still here?' her mother surprised her by asking.

She frowned. 'Yes. But——'

'Then everything will work out,' her mother nodded, her usual air of calm and tranquillity settling over her, just as if those few minutes of terror had never taken place.

Aura knew that look so well, accepting it because she had no other choice. 'Mummy, James is only human,' she tried to reason. 'We can all only hope now.'

'James will make sure everything works out,' her mother insisted lightly. 'He's a man who *makes* things happen.' She got out of bed. 'I'll just go down now and sit with Marmaduke.'

Aura frowned as she slowly followed her mother down the stairs. Her mother was endowing James with powers neither he, nor any other human being, possessed, and she was coming to rely on him completely to make her world a safe and tranquil thing. It was too great a responsibility to ask of anyone, let alone a man who had only known them for a week!

'All right?' James prompted softly as her mother sat on the floor crooning to the unconscious cat.

Aura still looked troubled. 'She has this idea that you can somehow make everything magically right.'

'I will,' he told her quietly. 'It's time you had someone to share a little of the responsibility.'

'You don't understand.' She shook her head. 'Marmaduke is still very sick, you heard what the vet said about the severity of the cuts and how weak he is; my mother could be expecting what amounts to a miracle.'

'Aura, we all have to hope for them sometimes.' His expression softened as he looked at her still-crooning mother. 'If love can cure him that cat will soon be out terrorising the neighbourhood again!'

Her face was still shadowed. 'And if it doesn't?'

'Have a little faith, Aura.' He touched her cheek gently. 'Sometimes it's all we have.'

The next twenty-four hours, the crucial time according to the vet, were absolute hell. When the cat woke up he was in so much pain that they called the vet out to him again. Aura's mother sat by him the whole time, refusing to leave him even to get dressed, Aura bringing her clothes down to her.

James insisted Aura open the shop the next day, only leaving them long enough to return to his apartment to change before coming back to spend the day with her mother.

'He's very nice,' said Jeanne when James had brought them both down a cup of tea.

'Very.' And after this, no matter what the outcome, she couldn't ask him to stay out of her life.

He was unique; how many other men in his position, with a very important business of their own to run, would take a day off from that to help them through the crisis of their injured cat? Even her father, the man she had adored, had been fallible. James had a strength that enveloped all about him.

With those odds on his side it was impossible for Marmaduke not to pass the danger point and begin to regain his strength; he wouldn't have dared do anything else! Aura sat beside her mother and wept when the cat got up and wobbled out of the basket he hadn't left for over a day to make his way to his food-bowl, looking up at them expectantly when he discovered it was empty. A light diet when he was up to it, the vet had instructed, and as Marmaduke liked nothing better than boiled fish, and received it only on special occasions, he quickly emptied the plate.

Aura left her mother and the cat together in the kitchen, going through to the lounge to tell James the good news. He sat alone, his eyes closed, and she stood for a moment just gazing her fill of him. She could love this man, could love his loving generosity, his tenderness. There wasn't a single thing about him that she couldn't love, that she *didn't* love, even that arrogance he occasionally displayed.

The colour drained from her face as she realised what a fool she had been. She *loved* James, had from the moment he had been so understanding about the way her mother was. She had known it was madness to become involved with him, she just hadn't been able to stay away. Oh God, what did she do now?

James's eyes flickered open, frowning his concern as he saw her pallor and the tears on her cheeks. 'I'm so sorry.' He quickly crossed the room to her side. 'The vet did warn us that there was only a fifty-fifty chance,' he comforted. 'You——'

'Marmaduke is fine,' she assured him stiltedly, evading his touch as she stepped back. 'He's been eating. I—I think you should go home and rest now. You look exhausted.'

'I'm not tired,' he dismissed, frowning as she moved about the room aimlessly picking up ornaments before putting them down again. 'Aura, what's wrong?'

He even *knew* too much about her, about the way she reacted to things, the way she *felt*. 'Nothing,' she told him abruptly. 'I just—the cat is out of danger now, and I think you should go and get some sleep.'

He sighed, those tell-tale grooves appearing and disappearing in his cheeks. 'You're asking me to leave?'

God, that sounded so ungrateful after all the help

he had given them. But he could *destroy* her and the life she had made here with her mother. 'I'm suggesting you go home and rest,' she carefully corrected.

'And never come back,' he rasped harshly. 'Aura, what did I do wrong between cooking dinner and now?'

After years of taking care of her mother and herself it had come as a shock to return upstairs after her day's work and find James in the kitchen cooking dinner and the table laid—for three.

She had felt a moment's resentment then, felt as if James was taking over and not merely trying to make a place for himself in her life. And then he had turned and smiled at her, taken her in his arms and kissed her, and that closed-in feeling had changed to anticipation.

*He* hadn't done anything wrong between dinner and now, *she* was the one who had realised she was in love with him!

'Don't be silly,' she dismissed coolly. 'It's just that Mummy and I can cope now, and——'

'And I'm no longer necessary,' he finished grimly, emerald clashing angrily with brown. 'I'd like to punch him on the nose.'

She gave a startled frown. 'Who?'

'The man who let you down when you needed him, so you've decided never to need anyone again,' James rasped, his eyes narrowed.

The pain in her chest was emotional, an aching reminder of how well this man had come to know her. 'It's a rule I never intend to break.' She met his gaze unflinchingly, knowing that if he didn't soon leave, her control would be shattered.

He drew in a ragged breath, fighting for control. 'A little at a time, Aura,' he reminded her.

She shook her head. 'You ask for too much.'

His eyes darkened with pain. 'So do you,' he said huskily. 'I *can't* give you up.'

'You never had me.'

'Oh, yes.' He stood in front of her now, gently caressing each side of her face. 'Briefly, like the touch of a butterfly, you were mine.' His thumbs softly touched her trembling mouth. 'Don't shut me out, Aura,' he pleaded.

She drew in a harsh breath. 'Can't you see that I have to?' she groaned, her eyes bright with unshed tears.

'The only thing you *have* to do at this moment is kiss me,' he encouraged raggedly. 'It's hours since I even touched you!'

He felt so good, *smelt* so good, a combination of aftershave and pure *James*—and he tasted just as good.

She could become addicted to his kisses, already knew the flat was going to seem empty without him.

'I'll just—oh! Oh,' her mother said lightly.

Aura's cheeks burnt as she broke away from James to turn to her.

Her mother beamed at them both. 'I just thought I would take Marmaduke upstairs in his basket so that we can both get some sleep. Please, don't let me interrupt you,' she said vaguely, carrying the sleeping cat up the stairs.

Aura turned back to James, her embarrassment fading as she saw the amusement in his eyes and the twitch of his mouth as he fought not to laugh. She tried to look stern, and failed miserably, smiling weakly. 'I always thought parents were supposed to object, not encourage you to carry on,' she said disgustedly.

'Have dinner with me tomorrow night?' he said huskily.

'Yes. No! I can't.' She shook her head, totally disconcerted by the unexpectedness of the invitation—as he had known she would be.

'I want to strangle him!' James grated with feeling. 'Come on, Aura, I'm only asking you out to dinner, not something disreputable.'

She gave a half-smile. 'Are you always this persistent?'

His mouth twisted. 'Only with the woman who is slowly driving me out of my mind!'

She felt a tremor of excitement at the admission. 'I really can't, James,' she choked.

'Is there something wrong with being seen out in public with me?' he rasped.

Not for any reason she would ever be able to tell him. She knew he wouldn't believe her if she told him so, but *he* was the one who could be embarrassed if anyone recognised her.

'My place,' he bit out. 'We can have dinner at my apartment.'

It was tempting, to be able to be with him knowing there was no chance of recognition. But she also knew she would be tempted into wanting more than just dinner.

'Your mother can come too,' he added desperately as she still didn't answer him.

Aura smiled at that. 'Mummy wouldn't go without Marmaduke in which case we might as well have dinner here.'

'I'll bring the wine——'

'No.' She sighed as he looked at her expectantly. 'I'll bring the wine. But on Saturday; tomorrow I keep the shop open late. So I'll bring the wine on Saturday night.'

Dark brows rose over amused green eyes. 'An independent woman?'

'You wouldn't think so from the last few days,' she said drily, strangely feeling an overwhelming relief now that the problem of whether or not she would see James again had been settled.

'I remember a very angry, very determined young woman visiting my office a week ago,' he gently mocked.

'I'm sure you were terrified,' she derided, doubting that anything unnerved this man, his quiet strength invincible.

'For a while I was,' he answered seriously, caressing her mouth. 'It's hard, letting yourself care again, isn't it?'

She swallowed hard, knowing he was trying to reassure her by revealing his own vulnerability. Maybe they were alike, both hurt by the past and afraid to trust the future. But James wasn't a man who would remain afraid of anything. What would they do if he fell in love with her too?

'That isn't what we're doing, James,' she dismissed distantly. 'We hardly know each other.'

'On Saturday we'll get to know all there is to know about each other,' he promised softly. 'You can tell me your life story, if you like.'

She stiffened, pulling away from him. 'I *don't* like! If that's one of the conditions for having dinner with you, then I——'

'It isn't.' He held up his hands defensively. 'God, Aura, why is it that being with you is like walking on eggshells the whole time? You only have to tell me what you want me to know,' he sighed at her unyielding expression. 'I'm not going to be taking down notes so that I can check their authenticity once you've gone. I'm certainly not interested in hearing about anyone you were involved with before we met,' he scowled.

Her mother was right, he was a possessive man. He was also the man she loved. How could she *not* love him? 'In that case, neither am I,' she returned lightly. 'When do you want me?' She knew it was the wrong thing to have said as soon as the words left her lips, his eyes darkening warmly. 'To arrive for dinner,' she clarified drily.

'Eight o'clock will be fine,' he replied with amusement. 'I'm going to leave now before you change your mind!'

'I can always pick up the telephone,' she reminded him.

'I'll refuse your calls like I did last time.' He shrugged unconcernedly.

'*This* time I would leave a message,' she warned him.

All the next day she told herself to pick up the telephone and do exactly that. But she couldn't do it. What if this were the last time she saw him? It *had* to be the last time. Wasn't every woman entitled to be with the man she loved when she said goodbye to him?

'You look lovely, darling.' Her mother looked up and smiled, the cat snoozing in his basket beside her as she watched television.

Aura was so nervous she was shaking with the tension, had changed her dress three times, finally settling on a pale green sheath of a gown that gave her the sophistication she felt would be needed to make the break from James final.

She frowned uncertainly. 'You're sure the two of you will be all right here on your own? If not just say so and I can——'

'Aura, Marmaduke and I will be just fine,' her mother assured her.

'I've left James's number on the pad beside the telephone. And——'

'Aura,' she was gently interrupted again. 'Will you just go out and enjoy yourself!'

She didn't doubt that her mother would cope perfectly well while she was gone; *she* was the one who was nervous. Going to James's apartment, the two of them alone, where no one could interrupt them, was not a sensible thing to be doing. Once again she thought of picking up the telephone and calling him to cancel their date.

The ringing of the doorbell startled her so much she dropped her clutch-bag to the floor, all the contents spilling out on to the carpet. Surely James hadn't anticipated her cowardice and come to get her after all?

'I'll answer it, dear,' her mother reassured her as she grovelled about on the floor searching for her missing lip-gloss.

Damn James. *Give* a little, he had said. Turning up in this way was *demanding*.

'Look who's here, Aura,' her mother announced lightly.

If James thought she was going with him after this he was sadly mistaken! She wouldn't——

'Aura?' her mother prompted again.

She grabbed the errant lip gloss from under the sofa and straightened, the colour fading from her flushed cheeks as she faced their visitor. Adrian ...

# CHAPTER FIVE

HANDSOME didn't begin to describe Adrian Mayhew; he had the sort of golden good looks a film-star or male model would envy, like a youthful Robert Redford with his blond hair that showed sunbleached highlights after his holiday as it fell with deliberate casualness across his brow, his blue eyes twinkling with good humour.

And he left Aura cold. Totally cold.

'Hi,' he greeted her softly, his gaze frankly admiring on her slender beauty in the pale green gown.

What was he doing here? Had he spoken to James? Did he know about the two of *them* seeing each other? More to the point, did James now know about her and Adrian!

'I'll just take Marmaduke through to the kitchen for his supper,' her mother put in gently, the two of them, Marmaduke in his cat basket, gone within seconds.

Aura stared at Adrian warily. What did he *want*?'

'What's wrong with the cat?' He arched blond brows.

'An accident,' she dismissed abruptly.

He shrugged. 'You're looking well,' he told her huskily, the beige suit he wore showing off his tan perfectly, his grin sparkling white against his bronzed skin.

'So are you,' she returned drily, relieved when her voice sounded normal.

He gave a dismissive shrug. 'There isn't much to do but sunbathe in Antigua.'

'Poor you,' she returned caustically. 'All that sun and clear blue sea must have been awful for you.'

He looked irritated. 'Didn't you wonder where I had got to?'

'No.' She was in complete control again now, moving from behind the sofa to face him.

His eyes hardened. 'You weren't interested in seeing me?'

She gave a disbelieving laugh. 'Certainly not.'

'But——'

'Adrian, I believe I made my feelings clear concerning seeing you again the last time we met,' she cut in harshly.

His face was flushed at the dismissal. 'But it's different now.'

Her eyes widened. 'Is it?'

'Aura, cut out the act and admit you've been desperate to contact me,' he rasped.

'I most certainly—ah,' her brow cleared, 'I forgot. So much has happened this last week that I completely forgot about that little problem with my lease.' She gave a weary sigh. 'That *is* what you're talking about, isn't it?'

'It certainly isn't a *little* problem,' Adrian looked furious. 'And how the hell could you forget about something like that?'

'Other—problems,' she evaded, her head back at his challenge. So much *had* happened since he had been away that she had forgotten her initial reason for meeting James; it certainly hadn't occurred to her that she would have to face a confrontation like this with Adrian, never imagining that he would come straight to see her on his return from his holiday without having first been to his office. She had been expecting anger from him at having his plan thwarted, not uninformed satisfaction on his part, believing he had her at a disadvantage. 'I presume you've come here to bargain?' she drawled.

He looked smug, like a man who was about to get his fondest wish—and without too much effort on his part. 'Crudely put, but——'

'True,' she finished drily. 'And what do you have to bargain *with*, Adrian?'

'You know damn well I can give you that lease—in return for the relationship you cheated me out of,' he said triumphantly.

'Did you think of this all by yourself or did someone have to help you?' she dismissed scathingly.

His eyes narrowed, his lips thinned. 'If you don't stop playing games with me you can forget all about your lease—no matter what you may feel inclined to offer,' he told her nastily.

'Tell me, Adrian,' she said slowly. 'Did your wife enjoy her holiday too?'

Some of the bravado deserted him, his expression suddenly wary. 'So, you know that I'm married.' He shrugged.

'Did your son go with you too, or is he still away at school?'

'What is this?' he demanded impatiently. 'OK, so I'm married and have a son; what does that have to do with us?'

'Nothing,' she assured him shruggingly. 'I just wondered if—Selina and Robert, isn't it?—enjoyed their holidays too?'

'Selina had a great time—as usual,' he scowled. 'My son is still at school. Now can we talk about your lease?'

She arched blonde brows. 'What about it?'

Adrian gave a low growl in his throat. 'You got the lawyers' letter!'

'Of course I got it,' she assured him. 'And when I saw your partner last week he was most apologetic about the mistake that had obviously been made,' she added.

'James?' he grated. 'You've discussed this with him?'

She nodded. 'Not only discussed it with him but *settled* it with him too.'

Adrian looked as if he had had the rug pulled out from under him. 'You have a new lease?' he asked.

'I do.' She gave an inclination of her head. 'I'm sorry if anticipating my distress, and my not being able to contact you, has sustained you through the terrible ordeal of a holiday in the Caribbean, but my lease is all legally renewed—and binding,' she added with satisfaction.

'James wouldn't—he couldn't——' Adrian gave her a sharp look. 'Did you tell him about us?'

'Us?' She arched brows. 'There isn't any us, and there never was. Now if you will excuse me, Mr Mayhew, I have an appointment this evening,' she said pointedly.

He clasped her arm, his grip painful. 'I want you, Aura!'

She shook off his restraining hand, her eyes flashing furiously. 'Don't *touch* me!' she hissed.

'Or what?' he challenged contemptuously.

Her breathing was agitated. 'I asked you to leave; which of us do you think would be the more embarrassed if I had to ask for official help to achieve that?' She met his gaze defiantly, hoping he wouldn't force her to carry out that challenge—because she would lose!

He stepped back. 'You're going to regret this, Aura, going to regret the day you went to my partner behind my back!'

She already regretted meeting James and falling in love with him! But it was Adrian's calm that worried her now. He was *too* calm in the face of defeat, had already proved he wasn't a man to make an enemy of.

'Goodbye, Adrian,' she said firmly.

His mouth twisted. 'I don't think so,' he drawled, giving her a mocking smile before taking his leave.

Aura leant weakly against the sofa, more shaken by the meeting than she wanted to acknowledge.

This confrontation had been nothing like she had imagined, sure Adrian wouldn't find out his plan had failed until he returned to his office and realised he had no further hold on her.

He was angry now, but if he ever found out she had

actually dated James ... How much more determined to have her would he be then?

God, he was dangerous.

How she wished she had never met Adrian. Or
James. How much more peaceful—and safe—her life
had been then!

'Aren't you going to be very late?'

She looked up at her mother's query, glancing
quickly at her wrist-watch, groaning when she saw it
was already after eight o'clock; James would be
wondering what had happened to her.

But she couldn't face him now, was too shaken
from her meeting with Adrian.

'I'm not going.' She shook her head. 'I—I'm not
feeling well.'

Her mother instantly looked concerned. 'What is
it, dear?'

'I—a headache,' she invented. 'I have a terrible
headache.'

Her mother frowned. 'Has Adrian upset you in
some way?'

'No, of course not. Although it was a little—
awkward, having him turn up here in that way,' she
excused herself.

'That's what I thought,' her mother nodded. 'Do
you want me to call James?'

'What for?' she said sharply.

'To tell him about your headache, of course.' She
looked puzzled by Aura's vehemence. 'He's sure to
be concerned.'

'I—no, I'll call him,' she decided, her palms damp.

She wasn't even going to be able to see James one last time!

James answered the telephone on the second ring, and she knew he had been anticipating her call.

'The cat's had a relapse. Your mother isn't feeling well. The shop has burnt to the ground,' he drawled after she had identified herself.

Aura stiffened. Was she such a coward? Yes, came the unhesitant reply, when it came to this man she was. And she couldn't bear his disappointment in her. 'I'm running a little late,' she told him coolly. 'I should be there in about twenty minutes.'

For a moment she thought he wasn't going to answer her, and then came his audible sigh of relief. 'I'll be waiting,' he told her gruffly.

Aura stared at the receiver for several minutes after she had softly replaced it. She didn't need the nagging little voice in the back of her head telling her she had made a mistake. Just as she didn't need the soaring of her heart to tell her she wanted this last evening with James desperately!

She stood up decisively, going through to the kitchen to see her mother. 'I'm going out after all. I— my headache's gone.' She faltered slightly over the deception.

'I'm glad,' her mother nodded. 'Have a nice time.'

Had she imagined it, or had there been a gleam of laughter in her mother's eyes at her about-face after talking to James?

Something strange, and wonderful, seemed to be happening to her mother, a slow return to awareness of the world about her. The signs were small, and could turn out to be insignificant, but they could also be the miracle Aura had hoped for.

She was so lost in thought that she barely registered the drive to James's apartment, suddenly finding herself outside his door, her heart beating an erratic tune in her chest.

God, she was so nervous, she had forgotten the promised wine! Was there an off-licence nearby that she could—of course she couldn't go off searching for an off-licence; she was already forty minutes late! She would just have to suffer James's teasing.

'I forgot——' Her apology lodged in her throat as she took in James's appearance, his masculinity hitting her like a force, knocking her breathless. His shirt and trousers were just as well tailored as all his other clothes, but the trousers emphasised the power of his thighs, and the shirt was unbuttoned at the throat to reveal the dark hair that grew in abundance on his chest. Aura instantly ached to touch him there.

'You forgot . . .?' he prompted gruffly.

'The wine,' she finished in a rush. 'I was already late, and——'

'Calm down, Aura.' He gently ushered her inside, his arms going about her as he kissed the lip gloss from her mouth. 'The wine was your idea,' he murmured. 'I just wanted you.'

She couldn't breathe, found it difficult to stand when he was this close to her. 'A promise is a promise,' she insisted weakly.

'You didn't promise, you offered,' he reminded her huskily. 'I thought you were going to let me down, you know.'

She drew in a ragged breath. 'Does that mean there isn't any dinner?' She fought for normality.

He smiled. 'If necessary I was going to come over and drag you here!'

Her brows rose. 'Isn't that a little caveman?' she drawled, her breathing finally returning to normal.

James shrugged. 'You bring out those feelings in me. Besides, I don't like it when people don't turn up when I've gone to the trouble of cooking a meal. It's very bad-mannered, you know.'

With his usual sensitivity, he was giving her time to regain her equilibrium after that breathtaking hello they had just shared.

He frowned suddenly. 'Dinner is going to be delayed slightly, I'm afraid. You see——'

'James, if this isn't convenient, I can always come back another time . . .' By the time the sentence came to an end the speaker had appeared in the hallway.

Adrian . . .

Aura felt the colour drain from her face, frozen to the spot as Adrian stared back at her in complete disbelief.

He must have come straight here from seeing her. Why? Had he been so worried about her meeting James last week that he had wanted to see exactly what his partner knew about the two of them?

His expression was changing from stunned amazement to icy anger, looking from her to James, and then back again. And obviously drawing his own conclusions from the situation.

Aura could feel his contempt, flinched from the knowing looks he was giving her, his thoughts all too obvious. He believed she had used her body to persuade James to renew her lease!

'Don't look so surprised, Adrian,' James drawled at his partner's silence, completely misinterpreting it in his ignorance of their past friendship. 'It is nearly nine o'clock on a Saturday evening; business finished hours ago.'

Adrian eyed Aura mockingly. 'Did it?' he said quietly. 'Of course it did,' he dismissed firmly, grinning at his partner. 'Forgive me, I was a little taken aback by the—beauty, of your date.'

Aura swallowed hard, her hands shaking as she wondered exactly what Adrian was going to tell James about *his* acquaintance with his date.

'I believe the two of you know each other,' James put in softly.

Aura gave a nervous start, and Adrian raised blond brows.

'We do?' he prompted slowly.

'Aura—Miss Jones, is one of our tenants,' James explained.

Aura's sigh of relief was covered by Adrian's agreement that the name did sound familiar to him.

'It should,' James drawled. 'You almost evicted her in your rush to get away last week.'

Adrian arched surprised brows. 'I did?'

'We can talk about it on Monday,' James dismissed. 'Right now Aura and I have a meal to eat,' he added pointedly. 'And Selina is probably waiting at home for you to take her out somewhere.'

'Ah yes, Selina.' Adrian eyed Aura speculatively as the puzzle of the source of her information about his family was answered. 'She's gone down to Kent to see Robert for the weekend. But I'm sure she would like to meet Miss Jones—if the two of you are free one evening next week?'

James shot Aura a frowning look. 'I'm not sure——'

'Perhaps we could let you know, Mr Mayhew,' she cut in tautly. 'I'm very busy at the moment.'

'Not in the evenings, surely?' he mocked.

Why was he doing this? He couldn't really want her to meet his wife, just as she knew he was furious about her being here with James.

'Stocktaking,' she supplied curtly.

'What sort of business is it that you have, Miss Jones?' he asked interestedly.

'Adrian,' James cut in patiently. 'I'm glad to know you had a good holiday and that I'll be seeing you in the office on Monday, but right now we have other plans,' he said again pointedly.

'Miss Jones is a business woman herself,' he drawled. 'I'm sure that she understands that after being away for ten days I'm—anxious to catch up on all the news.'

The evening had turned from a catastrophe into a disaster! It was obvious that Adrian *wasn't* going to tell James just how well he had known her in the past, but he was challenging her in such a way that it was impossible for her to retaliate. Adrian had back the advantage, and he knew it! If he should ever guess how deeply she had come to care for James he would make her life hell. If he wasn't going to already!

'That has to be a first,' James derided. 'Why don't

you call me tomorrow, Adrian?' he suggested drily.

'I wouldn't want to—interrupt—again.' Adrian looked at Aura as he spoke.

James's mouth tightened. 'You won't,' he rasped. 'Now—damn,' he muttered as a bell rang in the kitchen. 'I won't be a minute,' he promised Aura, giving his partner a frowning look before he had to leave them.

'Well, well, well,' Adrian predictably drawled once they were alone. 'I had no idea you were so— resourceful, my dear.'

Her head snapped back at the insult. 'Don't judge everyone by your own pitifully low standards!'

His eyes were cold. 'I suppose you're going to tell me you actually *like* James?'

Her cheeks were flushed with anger. 'Of course I like him!' she snapped.

'Enough to make sure he renewed your lease anyway,' he taunted.

'You——'

'I wouldn't.' His voice was dangerously soft as he grasped her wrist, her hand never making contact with his smug face. 'I think I should warn you, James has a low threshold for deceit,' he bit out coldly.

'I haven't——'

'Haven't you, *Miss Jones*?' he derided softly.

Her face burnt. '*You* were the one who acted as if you could never remember meeting me before,' she reminded him accusingly.

'And weren't you relieved?' he taunted.

'It would have been just as embarrassing for you as for me,' she said heatedly.

'I don't think so.' His thumb slowly caressed the inside of her wrist where he still held her. 'A man is allowed a few—indiscretions. It enhances—rather than detracts from his reputation.'

Aura paled, knowing all too well how easily a woman's reputation could be crushed. 'I got the impression your indiscretions had been far from a few.' She attacked rather than defending, freeing herself.

Adrian watched her with narrowed eyes. 'That can only make your involvement with me look worse in James's eyes.'

She knew that, oh God, she knew that! She had hoped to tell James tonight she wouldn't be seeing him again, was sure that he wasn't the type of man who talked about the women in his life, certain that Adrian would never learn from him of their brief friendship. And now this! How was she going to get out of this mess?

Adrian's confidence increased at her miserable silence. 'James is very hot on fidelity, you know,' he mocked. 'Other people's as well as his own.'

She didn't need to be told that James would be completely faithful to the woman lucky enough to be the recipient of his love. Why couldn't she have met him three years ago, even two years ago and it still wouldn't have been too late!

'I know all about that,' she said flatly.

'You do?' Adrian couldn't hide his surprise. 'You mean James—told you?'

If Adrian's father had been James's partner before him then she wasn't breaking any confidences by revealing what little she knew about James's broken engagement. 'He told me his engagement didn't work out, yes,' she confirmed abruptly.

'Didn't work out?' Adrian scorned. 'His fiancée was pregnant by another man!'

'Hot on fidelity' and a 'low threshold for deceit' hardly began to tell how deeply hurt James must have been by his fiancée's duplicity! 'Cheating', James had described it, but that hardly began to tell of the humiliation he must have suffered. He was such a proud man, so honest, that he must have suffered all the more because of that.

'It shows just how contemptible you are that you can find anything in the least amusing about the situation,' she snapped. 'Poor James.'

'Which brings us back to you,' Adrian taunted.

Her eyes flashed deeply brown. 'You know I knew nothing of your marriage *or* your son——'

'Let's talk about this some other time,' he murmured as James could be heard leaving the kitchen.

'No, I——'

'I'll call you,' Adrian added softly.

She hoped she didn't look as desperate as she felt, the smile she turned on James over-bright and lacking sincerity. She gave an inward groan of dismay as his eyes narrowed questioningly.

'Well, I'd better be on my way,' she heard Adrian say with some relief. 'And leave the two of you to enjoy your meal.'

'Go through and sit down,' James told her softly. 'I'll just see Adrian to the door.'

'I think I can find my own way,' Adrian drawled.

'Nevertheless,' James's voice was steely, 'I'll come with you.'

''Bye, Miss Jones,' Adrian called lightly. 'It's been a pleasure to meet you.'

Aura didn't so much sit down on the softly cushioned sofa as fall down, the soft murmur of the two men's voices barely audible to her, what they were actually saying not clear at all.

Had Adrian's car been parked outside? She hadn't seen it—if she had she would never had knocked on James's door so innocently! But then, she hadn't noticed much at all on the drive over here. Her life had taken such a downward turn the last couple of weeks; she had no idea where it was all going to end. She wasn't even sure that finishing with James would be enough to solve the problem now.

'Did he make a pass at you?'

She looked up sharply at the question, her cheeks flushed as she met James's troubled gaze. 'What do you mean?'

'You seemed—upset, when I came back from the kitchen?' he probed, striding over to stand in front of her. 'Adrian has a habit of flirting with every woman he meets, I wondered if he had said something to upset you.'

Adrian didn't need to *say* anything to upset her! 'No.' She straightened, meeting his gaze unflinchingly. 'Should I be insulted, do you think?' she added lightly.

'I *hoped* Adrian would have more sense than to step on my toes,' James said grimly.

'I'm sure he does,' she evaded. 'Are we going to eat now? I'm starving.' She wasn't even sure she would be able to get the food down her throat!

'It's all ready,' he nodded, still looking troubled. 'Aura, you would tell me if Adrian had insulted you in any way?'

She couldn't quite meet his gaze. 'Of course. This is a lovely room.' She looked around admiringly, noticing the comfortable elegance for the first time, the suite soft and informal, the colours of gold and brown very restful, the furniture once again big and solid; the person who had designed his office had obviously decorated his apartment too.

'I'm glad you like it.' He drily mocked her effort to change the subject. 'If Adrian should try to contact you——'

'You think he might?' She swallowed hard.

'I think it's quite within the realms of possibility,' he drawled. 'Tell me if he calls you.'

She frowned. 'Why have the two of you stayed partners when you obviously don't—get on?'

He shrugged, turning away. 'Why not? We just agree to differ, that's all. Now, madam, dinner is served,' he added lightly.

Maybe it was loyalty to Adrian's dead father that kept James partners with his son; whatever the reason, James wasn't prepared to talk about it. It seemed he had his share of secrets too.

What had it been like for him when he discovered his fiancée was expecting another man's child? She could imagine that only extreme circumstances could push him into using violence, and surely that had been one of them!

'You weren't really running late, were you?' he prompted as she pushed the prawns around in their sauce.

'Actually, I was—delayed,' she told him truthfully. 'How did you know I like prawns?'

'I asked your mother,' he said. 'You did intend coming tonight after all?'

'I did—intend coming,' she confirmed—even if she had changed her mind by the time she telephoned him. 'You asked my mother?' her brows were raised.

'Mm, which is why we have chicken for our main course; she told me it's your favourite,' he smiled. 'I was sure you would try to change your mind about tonight,' he admitted gruffly. 'I even went out today so that I couldn't take your call if you made one. When you telephoned earlier I——'

'Don't, James.' She put her hand on his, hating the look of vulnerability on his face. 'Please don't care for me.'

He smiled. 'Don't you know it's already too late for that?'

'James——'

'I care for you, Aura,' he told her huskily. 'I won't go into how much because I don't want to scare you off.'

She put her fork down in the bowl, drawing in a steadying breath, 'James, I——'

'I know,' he sighed. 'You aren't ready for that, yet. But I know something you are ready for.'

She looked at him sharply, swallowing hard. This man knew her so well, more than she would have wished, did he also know that every time she looked at him she ached with wanting him?

'What?' she asked in a hushed voice.

He stood up, and Aura's gaze followed him warily. If he should try to make love to her now she would melt ...!

He bent over her, his lips lightly brushing her cheek, seemingly by accident, but Aura was sure it was by design, her breath once more lodged in her throat.

'You're ready for—the next course.' He straightened, kissing her hard on the mouth before turning away, once again taking control for both of them as he saw her complete vulnerability.

# CHAPTER SIX

LISTENING to John Denver music always made Aura want to cry. His songs were beautiful and sad in turns, and anyone who couldn't see that beauty didn't appreciate good music, in her opinion. It came as no surprise to her that James possessed every cassette the talented songwriter and singer had ever made.

Tonight the sad songs seemed so personal, the beautiful ones so poignant, that Aura had trouble containing the tears.

She and James sat together on the sofa, her head resting on his chest as his arm lay across her shoulders.

After his verbal seduction of her at the dinner-table she had eaten the rest of her meal without really tasting it but knowing it was delicious anyway, the wine James provided adding to the light-headed feeling that had crept over her as he kept up the light-hearted bantering as they continued to eat.

She was filled with a fierce desperation as the meal ended, the hours slipping away too fast, as they always did when you wished time would simply stop in the place you were happiest.

They had talked about their childhoods, James's privileged one with parents who had obviously adored him and had been taken from him in a tragic accident when he was only twenty-one, her own childhood spent living in the country with parents who perhaps gave too much of their love to each other and not enough to the child that love had created, their love for each other an overwhelming emotion that consumed them.

Aura hadn't meant to tell James quite so much of the loneliness she had often felt as a child, but she knew that he was astute enough to have guessed at the things she hadn't told him, that the way her mother was now testified to the deep love she had felt for Aura's father.

She shouldn't have chosen John Denver when James asked her preference in music, should have chosen something more cheerful. She was going to be blubbering all over him like a baby in a moment!

Her eyes were swimming in tears as she looked up at him, and she saw his fierce frown of concern before his head bent to her hungry mouth.

Only tonight. It was all she had. Just tonight.

The words went round and round in her head, blinding her to caution, deafening her to sensibility. She wanted only to be with this man.

But was one night going to be enough? Would she be able to say goodbye after that?

'Aura?' James groaned at the uncertainty flickering across her revealing face.

It wouldn't be enough! With sudden clarity she knew that only a lifetime would be enough with this man, that he would demand it all.

'James, I——'

'No!' He towered over her like an avenging angel

as he laid her back against the sofa. 'Don't say it. Don't say anything. Just let me kiss you. Love you, as I've been longing to do.'

His mouth was fierce against her, his caresses sure and determined, and after only the briefest of hesitations, Aura returned that hunger.

His skin was like rasping satin as she smoothed the unbuttoned shirt from his shoulders, finally able to give in to her impulse to entangle her fingers into the dark hair curling on his chest, the hair soft and silky rather than wiry as she had imagined it would be, and she lowered her mouth to caress him.

He felt wonderful, steel and velvet, her lips touching him as her tongue tasted him, feeling him shudder beneath her caresses, his breath a ragged rasp in his throat, a throat that moved spasmodically as she kissed him there.

She wanted him, and now she knew that she needed him too.

There was nothing gentle about him tonight, and Aura revelled in his savagery, returning his kisses with equal demand, her throat arching as his lips travelled its length to the warm swell of her breasts visible above her gown.

His mouth was warm and moist, loving every inch of her, becoming impatient when he couldn't locate the zip at her spine, his eyes very dark when he looked up at her with mute appeal.

Her fingers shook slightly as she eased the zip down at her side, their gazes locked as James removed the dress completely and dropped it to the floor.

It had never been so important that her body be

beautiful, but as she looked into James's eyes she knew she was perfect to him, the cream satin teddy so sheer it was like a translucent skin over her pink-tipped breasts and the gentle mound of her womanhood.

A flush darkened his cheeks as, sitting back, he touched her, watching in fascination as her breasts became taut with need at his gentle caress, her breathing shallow as his hand sloped down to her hips and thighs, feeling the dampness there.

She closed her eyes as the memory of his long muscular legs beneath white shorts as he faced her across the tennis court came to mind, but this time they were entangled with hers, bronze against ivory.

Her eyes were the warmth of sherry when she opened them again, James's chest bare, only the fitted trousers stopping her fantasy from being reality.

She gasped as wet satin clung to her breast, giving a tortured groan as a hard tongue flicked over the sensitive nipple, a whimper of ecstasy escaping her parted lips as the razor-edge of his teeth bit down gently.

She had to touch him, had to know him as he was knowing her, her hair a blonde curtain about her face as she forced him down on the sofa cushions, following the path of that satiny hair as it left his chest in a V pattern down to the fastening of his trousers.

His manhood bulged against the straining material, and he gave a ragged groan as Aura touched him wonderingly, offering no resistance as she freed him to her waiting caresses.

He was magnificent naked, firmly muscled, his skin that rough velvet all over except where he was pure velvet, and it was there that she allowed him no respite.

The straps of her teddy slipped down her arms, the scrap of material disappearing as if by magic, their bodies burning as they touched from lips to ankles.

James lay above her, pressing her back into the cushions, not crushing her as she had thought he would, his thighs throbbing hotly against her as he sought entry.

'I—it's been a long time,' Aura found the courage to murmur.

He looked at her with loving eyes. 'I won't hurt you, darling.'

She longed to know that hardness of him inside her, but as she moved against him impatiently he held back, suddenly moving away from her completely to sit on the edge of the sofa, his back towards her.

Aura felt bereft, chilled without the warmth of his body beside her. 'James ...?'

'Don't touch me!' he groaned as she would have reached out to him.

What had happened? What had she done wrong?

James gave a low moan of regret as he turned to see the self-condemnation in her eyes. 'It wasn't you, Aura,' he hastened to reassure her, smoothing her tangled hair back from her face. 'I was about to do something we would both have regretted.'

'No——'

# Say  to romance

## AND YOU'LL GET

- •4 FREE BOOKS
- •1 FREE BRONZE-AND-ROSEWOOD LETTER OPENER
- •1 FREE SURPRISE

**NO RISK • NO OBLIGATION**
**NO STRINGS • NO KIDDING**

# *Say yes to free gifts worth over $20.00*

***Say YES*** to a rendezvous with romance, and you'll get 4 classic love stories—FREE! You'll get an elegant bronze letter opener—FREE! And you'll get a delightful surprise—FREE! These gifts carry a total value of over $20.00—but you can have them without spending even a penny!

MONEY-SAVING HOME DELIVERY!

***Say YES*** to Harlequin's Home Reader Service® and you'll enjoy the convenience of previewing 8 brand-new books every month, delivered right to your home before they appear in stores. Each book is yours for only $2.24—26¢ less than the retail price, plus 89¢ postage and handling per shipment.

SPECIAL EXTRAS—FREE!

You'll also get additional free gifts from time to time as a token of our appreciation for being a home subscriber.

***Say yes*** to a Harlequin love affair. Complete, detach and mail your Free Offer Card today!

# *FREE—bronze-and-rosewood letter opener*

As a bonus for saying YES to romance, we'll give you this beautiful letter opener as a GIFT! Elegant, with a lovely, supple blade, this bronze letter opener has a dainty rosewood handle. It will make your correspondence a romantic experience! This is FREE as our gift of love.

---

# Harlequin Home Reader Service®

# FREE OFFER CARD

**4 FREE BOOKS**

**FREE GIFTS FROM TIME TO TIME**

Place YES
sticker here

**FREE LETTER OPENER**

**FREE SURPRISE**

Please send me 4 Harlequin Presents® novels, free, along with my free letter opener and surprise gifts as explained on the opposite page.

308 CIH U1CT

Name _____
(PLEASE PRINT)

Address _____ Apt _____

City _____

Province _____ Postal Code _____

Offer limited to one per household and not valid for present subscribers. Prices subject to change.

PRINTED IN U.S.A.

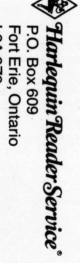

'Aura, I have never yet made love to a woman to stop her from leaving me,' he rasped. 'And I'm not going to start now, with you!'

Understanding flooded her, knowing that minutes ago he to had been filled with the same desperation that she had known all evening before he kissed her.

She hated the vulnerability in his eyes, despised herself for reducing him to what amounted to begging. He had already been hurt so much in the past; she didn't have the right to deny him the happiness they could have together, even if it were only briefly!

He gave a ragged sigh. 'I was seducing you into accepting a relationship you obviously aren't ready for——'

'James,' she came up on her knees beside him. 'If you'll accept me as I am, if you realise that this—may not be for ever, but just enjoy what we have now, I——' She broke off, remembering the threat in Adrian's eyes. 'There are things, in my past, that I'm not proud of,' she began again. 'As long as you can accept that they don't affect us, here and now, I'd like to see you again.' She held her breath, knowing she was asking for a lot.

His eyes darkened. 'Tomorrow?'

She swallowed hard. 'You do understand about—about the past?' she persisted. 'That no matter what you might—hear about me, that none of it affects how I feel about you now?'

He gave a teasing smile. 'Are you a mass-murderer?'

'James, you have to tell me that you can accept

that,' she told him earnestly. 'Or I won't be able to see you again.'

His arms closed about her fiercely. 'Don't you know I would promise you anything to keep you with me!'

She gave a choked cry. 'Then can we take here and now——'

'And tomorrow,' he put in lightly.

'And tomorrow,' she confirmed shakily. 'And forget about the past and the future?'

He looked down at her searchingly. 'You know that if you ever want to talk to me that I'll gladly listen?'

She nodded. 'Unfortunately I'm not the only one involved,' she revealed heavily. 'And some things are better left as they are.'

'Hm.' He sounded doubtful but resigned. 'Now that the mood has been well and truly broken,' he drawled self-derisively, 'we had better try and untangle our clothes and get dressed!'

Aura blushingly became aware of their nakedness, knowing by James's rueful expression that he had forgotten about it too during the gravity of their conversation.

'Has the mood been broken?' she said wistfully.

He smiled. 'I'm afraid so.'

'Pity,' she murmured as they dressed, knowing by the heat of James's gaze as he followed her movements when she pulled on her clothes that the desire had far from faded. But he was right, the mood had gone, and with it the desperation. They had time now; how much, with Adrian so threateningly in the background, she wasn't sure. But maybe as far as Adrian was concerned it was time to stop running.

After the abrupt end to their lovemaking there should have been awkwardness between them, but as they sat drinking coffee together Aura knew they were closer together than ever. James could be the other half of herself, maybe soon she would be able to tell him of the scandal two years ago, trust him with the truth, and hope he would understand. If Adrian didn't tell him about the two of them first! She was sure he wouldn't do that before he had spoken to her first, otherwise he would lose his advantage a second time.

'Maybe I'm old-fashioned,' James murmured as he took her in his arms at the door. 'But there's something not quite right about seeing a woman off at my door and then letting her drive herself home!'

Aura laughed softly. 'You *are* old-fashioned—and I love it!'

'You don't mind that chivalry isn't dead, then?' he asked.

She shook her head. 'I'd much rather a man opened a door for me than slam it in my face!'

His mouth twisted. 'I believe most women would!'

'Come to lunch tomorrow,' she invited him impulsively. 'Mummy will love it.'

'Only your mother?' he drawled.

'You can help me cook,' Aura mocked.

Her euphoria lasted until after James had walked down to her car with her and watched as she drove off. Then the heaviness of guilt settled upon her. She could be leaving James open to more hurt than refusing to see him again after tonight would have done. They said a short sharp break was the best way; wasn't she just prolonging the agony? But how was she supposed to tell the man she loved she could never see him again! She just wasn't that strong, had lost too much from her life already that mattered to her. Besides, Adrian didn't have the complete advantage, not when he was a married man with a son. And the past was still her secret, neither man knew about that.

'This is nice, dear,' her mother murmured softly as they set the table together in readiness for James's arrival.

Aura's smile was strained, the night-time hours having taken their toll on her decision to continue seeing James in spite of Adrian's veiled threats.

'It's been so long since there were three of us sitting down together for Sunday lunch,' her mother continued brightly, insensitive to Aura's worried silence. 'It will almost be like being a normal family again,' she added wistfully.

'We were never a *normal* family, Mummy,' Aura snapped before she could stop herself, at once contrite as she saw the hurt confusion on her mother's face. 'I'm sorry,' she sighed, 'That was completely uncalled for.'

Her mother looked troubled. 'Did your father and I make you feel so shut out?'

Aura held her breath. It was the first time her mother had spoken of her father in the past tense, almost as if she finally realised . . . 'You couldn't help loving each other as deeply as you did,' she said absently, almost afraid to hope, but wishing—oh God, *wishing* her mother would remember and accept that the man she loved was dead. She had seemed so much better lately, actually remembering to do things, maybe——Her hopes were dashed as her mother turned away, that vague look back in her eyes.

'Marmaduke will be waiting for his lunch,' she murmured as she wandered off without finishing the table.

Aura's breath left her in a shaky sigh. For a moment, for a very brief moment, she had begun to believe this nightmare were over.

She was beginning to doubt it ever would be.

James seemed to be watching her closely as they ate lunch together, and maybe she was talking too brightly, her laugh a little too forced; why not, she felt as if she were balancing on a tightrope, not knowing which way she was going to fall, but knowing the fall would be inevitable!

'As you're going to Helen's later, could you take over the jumpers I finished knitting for the children?' her mother requested as Aura and James returned from the kitchen after finishing the washing-up.

Aura gave a start. 'I hadn't intended——'

'Helen is the friend with Jonathan, isn't she?' James cut in mildly, totally at ease in their company.

'Yes, but——'

Her mother looked vague. 'Did I forget to mention that Helen telephoned last night and invited you over today, dear?'

She drew in an angry breath. 'You know you did,' she snapped with uncharacteristic impatience for her gentle mother.

'I'd like to go—if your friend wouldn't mind my tagging along?' James put in softly.

Helen meet James? She trusted her friend enough not to say anything out of turn, but even so . . . !

'Oh, Helen won't mind in the least,' her mother answered serenly. 'She's been matchmaking for Aura since they were children.'

He smiled. 'Am I to take it you think she will approve of me for Aura?'

'Of course she will.' Her mother returned his smile. 'How could she not?'

His smile faded, his brows raised as he met Aura's impatient gaze. 'Aura?' he prompted.

'Why not?' she snapped irritably. 'Helen will be expecting me.'

Her mother looked hurt by her sharpness. 'I really am sorry I forgot to mention Helen's call,' she said beseechingly. 'It was so late when you got home last night, and when you told me James was coming to lunch today I completely forgot about everything else but that.'

Aura's cheeks were red from the mention of last night, and she felt guilty for snapping at her mother in that way. 'It doesn't matter,' she smiled reassuringly. 'We can go over in a few minutes.'

'Meg?' James encouraged.

'Oh, I won't go,' she dismissed vaguely, standing up. 'I'll just sew two buttons on the neck-openings of the jumpers.' She went upstairs to get them.

Aura uncomfortably avoided James's searching gaze, knowing he was puzzled by her mood.

'If you would rather I didn't go with you . . .?' he finally said.

'Of course not,' she sighed, shaking off her mood of irritability. 'As long as you don't mind the teasing we'll no doubt get from Simon—Helen's husband,' she added drily.

'I'd like to meet your friends, Aura,' he told her quietly.

'And I'm sure they would love to meet you,' she returned brittly.

'Aura——'

'Here we are.' Her mother came back into the room. 'I wasn't long, was I?' she said brightly.

Her mother's reappearance was perfect timing as far as Aura was concerned. 'I'll give Helen your love.' She took the jumpers, knowing the children were going to love the pattern of one of their favourite television characters knitted into the front.

'Maybe she could bring the children over to see me some time soon,' her mother said.

'I'm sure she will.' Aura gave her mother an impulsive hug, knowing she had been awful to her today.

'She never goes out, does she?'

Aura turned sharply to James as he spoke quietly beside her in the car. 'Sorry?' she delayed.

'Meg,' he bit out abruptly. 'She never leaves the flat, does she?'

'Of course she—no,' she admitted heavily as he

gave her a reproving look.

'Never?'

She drew in a ragged breath. 'No. She doesn't have a phobia about going outside or anything like that,' she explained softly. 'The doctors believe it's just another way of shutting out the world without my father; if she doesn't go out in it she doesn't have to acknowledge that he isn't out there, somewhere. It's been that way since we moved to the shop, but the memories at the house were even worse for her when she couldn't understand why my father didn't come home!' She trembled as James's hand covered hers. 'The doctors believed it would be best if she were taken away from there, and she did seem to get better physically. But she never leaves the flat,' she acknowledged flatly.

'I wish there were something I could do to help you,' he spoke gruffly.

'Me?' She expressed surprise. 'But—I manage,' she sighed as he gave her another reproving look. 'Just being with you helps.' She stared down at their hands as she linked her fingers with his. 'I'm sorry I've been such a shrew today.'

His thumb caressed her palm. 'Feeling better now?'

She smiled gratefully at his lack of recrimination. 'Much,' she nodded.

'Tell me about Helen and Simon,' he prompted lightly. 'And of course Jonathan and the new baby.'

She knew it was a way of diverting her, of helping her forget whatever was worrying her. And it worked. She couldn't stay distant when she talked of her two godchildren, or told him how Simon had dispelled all Helen's doubts about marrying him after only knowing him a week by showering a vanful of her favourite chocolate bars on her. Helen had decided that anyone who cared enough to find out her secret passion had to be in love with her!

'You told him,' Helen complained to Aura after James had had difficulty containing his humour during their introduction.

'I——'

'I am sorry,' James chuckled. 'You'll have to tell me if Aura has any secret addictions like that; I need all the help I can get.'

Helen gave him an appreciative look. 'If you get any more help no female will be safe!'

'Hey,' Simon complained. 'You're a married woman.'

'And thanks to Aura, James knows my secret,' she taunted. 'Besides, haven't I had to suffer the two of you flirting right under my nose for years?'

James was an instant hit with Helen and Simon, as Aura had known he would be, and he didn't try to entice the children to sit on his knees; they just gravitated to him. Cats *and* children; what chance did she have to resist him?

She stood up to help when Helen suggested making them all a cup of tea.

'Uh oh,' Simon groaned. 'We may as well take the kids out into the garden, James; when these two women get into a huddle they don't surface for hours!'

James stood up with Annie still in his arms,

Jonathan already searching for his football. 'What do you suppose they find to talk about?' he asked drily.

'Oh, recipes, things like that,' Simon said tongue-in-cheek, sliding back the glass door that led out into the garden.

'I'm sure.' James joined in the teasing.

'Men!' Helen muttered as she moved about the kitchen. 'They won't even let you have a good gossip in peace!'

Aura chuckled softly. 'What is it you have to say about James?'

'And you're no better,' Helen reproved. 'Last weekend you told me James was a good man, an honest one—you didn't tell me how handsome or exciting he was!'

'He's handsome and exciting,' she reported obediently.

'I can *see* that,' Helen groaned. 'You aren't still thinking about not seeing him again?'

She grimaced. 'I'm not thinking at all,' she sighed. 'I can't be!'

'But——'

'Helen, he's Adrian's partner,' she cut in dully.

Her friend's eyes widened. 'Oh.' She frowned. 'Well that doesn't have to make a difference,' she dismissed. 'Adrian was the one who tried to buy you with diamonds——'

'Adrian is married with a son,' she interrupted again.

Helen's brows were lost beneath her feathered fringe. 'The lousy—well, that still doesn't have to affect you and James; you had no idea Adrian was married.'

'After the scandal two years ago, who would believe that?' she sighed.

'James would,' Helen said with instant certainty.

She shook her head. 'He would try to,' she acknowledged. 'But he was hurt years ago, and—I think he might find it hard to trust, no matter how much he wanted to.'

'It wasn't your fault——'

'Maybe if I thought he loved me I could tell him,' she sighed. 'But even then it would be difficult for any man to accept. And we've only known each other ten days!'

'He does care for you,' Helen insisted.

'I know,' she accepted flatly. 'But I'm not sure it's enough to understand all this. He deserves someone who can love him without reserve, without these complications.'

'But it's you he wants,' Helen reasoned.

Aura straightened. 'I learnt very early in life that we can't have something just because we wish for it.' Bitterness edged her voice.

'Aura——'

'Come on, let's get the tea ready and prove to the men that we don't have to gossip all day.' She ignored her friend's hurt look, knowing she couldn't talk about her feelings for James any more today.

Simon raised his brows when they joined them out in the garden a few minutes later. 'I guess you weren't as interesting a subject as I thought you were, old man,' he drawled.

'Come and have your tea,' Helen instructed her husband while James looked searchingly at Aura.

She avoided his gaze, only relaxing again when they all joined in a game with the two excited children.

James was very quiet on the drive back to her home, and she knew it was her fault. But she couldn't change the way she was, or the sudden mood changes that could attack her at any time. He had asked for a little at a time, and that was exactly what she was giving him.

'I liked them very much,' he finally said.

'They liked you too,' she said unnecessarily.

'Was there some reason why you refused to make a definite agreement to go over to dinner with them this week?'

A blush darkened her cheeks. 'I thought we should talk about it first,' she dismissed. 'Helen did rather put us on the spot.'

'I would have enjoyed it,' James told her softly.

She shrugged. 'Well, there's still time to let them know we can go over one evening. Just let me know——'

'Aura, they were only being friendly; my getting to know the people you care about isn't committing you to anything.'

She drew in a ragged breath. 'I thought—we don't know each other well enough to socialise with each other's friends!'

He was suddenly distant, although Aura was sure he hadn't moved away from her in the confines of the car. 'Of course,' he accepted abruptly. 'Well, I've enjoyed today, Aura; can I see you one night in the week?'

She had hurt him again, something she seemed to be able to do all too easily. 'James, try to understand——'

'I'm trying to,' he rasped. 'Could we have dinner? Tuesday, perhaps?'

'Yes,' she accepted in a small voice, feeling about as small.

He stopped the car beside the pavement, leaving the engine idling. 'I won't come up,' he bit out. 'I have some papers I need to look through before tomorrow.'

The kiss he gave her lasted barely long enough for her to be conscious of his lips on hers, his eyes shadowed with pain as he moved back to his own side of the car.

'I'll call you,' he said instantly.

Ten days. She had known him ten days, and in that time he had become as much a part of her life as all the other things she cared about. He didn't call her the next day, and Adrian didn't come to see her either. Adrian's absence she could live with, guessing he was doing it intentionally, letting her worry a little in return for thwarting him the last time. But not even talking to James on the telephone seemed strange to her, as if part of her were missing, a very essential part.

By Tuesday afternoon she was so angry with herself and everyone else that she buried herself in the stock-room out of everyone's way. Even her business didn't hold her attention as it usually did, and she had to go back and count several items more than once when she realised she had put a ridiculous figure in the amount column.

'Someone to see you, Aura,' Jeanne called up the stairs.

She bumped her head on the shelf above as she straightened too fast. James! He had come to see her about tonight instead of calling her!

But there was only a woman standing in the shop, a tall, elegant woman with glossy black hair smoothed back in a chignon, her beautiful face deeply tanned, making her eyes look violet rather than the deep blue they really were.

Without needing an introduction, Aura knew instinctively who this woman was. Selina Mayhew . . .

# CHAPTER SEVEN

AURA didn't know how she knew the identity of her visitor, but somehow she was sure that was who the other woman was.

What was she doing here? Had she found out about Aura's brief friendship with Adrian and come to confront her about it?

Maybe she was wrong, maybe this wasn't really Adrian's wife but a customer looking for a particular product. Maybe——

As the woman put up a hand to straighten her already smooth hair, unaware of Aura's presence yet, Aura saw the bracelet and knew she wasn't mistaken. It was the diamond bracelet Adrian had offered *her* for her birthday!

Unless it was one exactly like it? No, she accepted heavily, it was the same bracelet, its intricate design was indelibly printed on her memory. And Adrian had given it to his wife after *she* refused to accept it. What sort of man was he to give his wife the cast-off of a proposed mistress? She knew the answer to that question all too well!

She smoothed her hands down her hips, taking a deep breath. 'Can I help you?'

The woman turned to look at her, and Aura saw just how dazzlingly beautiful she was. Her skin was as smooth as satin, long lashes fringing those violet eyes, her nose small and straight, a rose lip-gloss outlining

the perfection of her pouting mouth, the designer-
label gown of cream silk suiting her slender body
perfectly. Why on earth did Adrian chase after other
women when he had a wife as beautiful as this at
home?

'Miss Jones?'

Even her voice was beautiful, pitched low and soft,
the sort of voice that made men drool. 'That's right,'
she confirmed distantly.

'I'm Selina Mayhew,' she introduced herself
lightly, holding out her hand.

She accepted the gesture, nodding abruptly. 'Mrs
Mayhew.'

'Selina, please,' she invited. 'I believe we have a
mutual acquaintance.'

Aura stiffened, glancing uncomfortably towards
Jeanne. If this woman was going to start spouting
accusations she certainly didn't want an audience to
it.

'I'll go and finish off the stock-taking,' Jeanne
offered tactfully.

'Thank you,' Aura accepted gratefully.

Selina Mayhew smiled warmly at Jeanne as she
made her departure. Aura watched the other woman
warily, wondering how she had found out about her.

She was so *beautiful*, her features perfect, and
although she must be about thirty, the same as
Adrian, to have a nine-year-old son, she looked no
older than her early twenties at most.

'A mutual acquaintance?' Aura prompted abruptly once they were alone.

'Yes.' The other woman included her in the

warmth of her smile. 'James,' she supplied as Aura still looked wary.

*James!* What on earth did James have to do with this?

Selina Mayhew gave a husky laugh. 'Who did you think I meant?'

Aura searched for any double meaning to the innocently put question, but the other woman looked genuinely puzzled by her behaviour. She didn't *know* about her involvement with Adrian. Aura relaxed slightly.

'Selina *Mayhew*,' she feigned realisation. 'The wife of James's partner?'

'That's right,' the other woman beamed. 'Have you met Adrian?'

Had they *met*? Almost too intimately! 'He was at James's apartment when I arrived the other evening,' she supplied distantly.

'Was he?' Selina Mayhew frowned. 'Concerning work, probably,' she nodded. 'The poor dear has been most distracted while we were away.'

Aura guessed that Adrian's preoccupation had little to do with thoughts of work and more to do with her downfall! 'I believe they were discussing business,' she said truthfully.

'I hope Adrian didn't spoil your evening?' the other woman sympathised. 'Time doesn't seem to have any meaning for him when there's work to be done.'

Surely this woman didn't believe her husband actually *worked late* on those evenings he didn't get home? Her completely guileless expression said that she did!

'He left shortly after I arrived.' Aura avoided mentioning just how badly he had 'spoilt her evening'.

'Well, I'm glad the two of you have met,' Selina Mayhew beamed. 'It makes what I have to ask you much easier.'

Aura stiffened warily. 'Oh?'

'Yes,' the other woman nodded warmly. 'You see, Saturday is our tenth wedding anniversary——'

'Congratulations,' Aura drawled.

'Thank you,' Selina Mayhew smiled. 'We're having a party for a few friends, and of course we want James to be there.'

'Of course,' she acknowledged, her wariness increasing.

'So now you can see my problem,' the other woman said brightly.

'Er—no.' She shook her head. 'I don't see it at all.'

Selina Mayhew gave a puzzled frown. 'Maybe I haven't explained myself very well,' she sighed. 'James called me last night and told me that as you don't like to go to parties he wouldn't be coming either.'

The fact that he was right didn't alter the fact that she had never mentioned disliking parties to James. But she *had* told him she didn't think they knew each other well enough to socialise with each other's friends! And he had refused this woman's invitation because of that, she was sure of it.

'We have no arrangements to meet on Saturday,' she said coldly.

'James refuses to come without you.' The other woman shrugged.

Aura's mouth tightened. 'I think you should talk to James about this; I didn't even know he had been invited to a party on Saturday.'

'Oh dear.' Selina Mayhew looked contrite. 'I hope I haven't upset you by coming here.'

'Not at all,' she dismissed briskly. 'As I said, I have no knowledge of the party beyond what you've told me. Perhaps James has reasons of his own for refusing?'

The other woman looked hurt by the idea. 'He told me the woman he was dating doesn't like crowds,' she insisted.

'And, as I just said, he hasn't even invited me,' Aura said.

The other woman brightened. 'Does that mean that if he does ask you you'll come?'

'No,' she sighed. 'It doesn't mean that at all.'

'But there aren't going to be crowds of people there,' Selina Mayhew encouraged. 'Just a few close friends.'

'Like James,' she said heavily.

'I can't imagine having an anniversary party without him there,' she said. 'That's why I thought I would come and invite you personally, explain to you how important this is to Adrian and me. Beside the fact that we're all friends, it would look very odd if Adrian's business partner didn't attend,' she frowned.

Appearances, James and the Mayhews all lived in a world where that was all-important. Although it obviously wasn't as important to James as to the others; he had refused the invitation because of her.

'You don't even have to stay long if you don't want

to,' the other woman encouraged. 'James isn't known for his socialising qualities.'

'I don't——'

'Oh, please come,' she urged Aura. 'I'm sure you'll enjoy yourself.'

It would probably be worth it just to see Adrian's face, surely he wouldn't dare make a scene at his own anniversary party! But it was a risk she dared not take.

'I really am sorry, Mrs Mayhew.' She spoke firmly. 'As I said, James hasn't even invited me.'

'Then I'll have to make sure he does.' She brightened, holding out her hand. 'I do hope we'll meet again on Saturday,' she beamed.

Aura felt shaken after the other woman's departure. How could that nice woman be married to such a lecher? She certainly didn't deserve the husband fate had dealt her.

'*Adrian* Mayhew's wife?' Jeanne rejoined her.

'Yes,' she sighed.

'A wife you knew nothing about,' Jeanne said with certainty.

'Oh, Jeanne,' she gave the other woman a shaky smile. 'I wish everyone had your trust.'

'Did she give you a rough time?' Jeanne frowned.

'She came to invite me to accompany James to the party she and Adrian are having on Saturday for their tenth wedding aniversary,' Aura answered a little hysterically.

Her assistant nodded slowly. 'It figures.'

Aura blinked. 'Sorry?'

'I would watch out for Selina Mayhew if I were you,' Jeanne advised thoughtfully. 'She reminds me of that plant that devours flies, innocent enough from a distance, but if you get too close you're dead.'

'Jeanne!' She looked at her friend wonderingly.

'Believe me,' the other woman warned. 'No woman—wife, meekly accepts her husband's indiscretions without thought of some retribution.'

'She doesn't know about Adrian and me,' Aura told her drily.

Jeanne's brows rose. 'Are you sure about that?'

'Of course I—she would hardly invite me to her party if she did know,' Aura dismissed confidently.

'Nevertheless, I would watch out for her,' Jeanne warned again.

'I think you've been reading too many whodunits,' Aura lightly teased her friend's addiction. 'In this case, no one did it!'

'I hope you're right.' Jeanne didn't sound at all convinced.

There had been nothing in the least offensive or accusing about Selina Mayhew, she had been pleasantly friendly, with no undertones of resentment in her manner at all; Jeanne had to have been mistaken.

She distractedly answered the telephone as it rang. 'Yes?'

'Aura?'

James! Her hand tightened on the receiver. 'Yes.' She was wary now.

'Is our dinner date still on for tonight?' he asked distantly.

'Unless you want to cancel it,' she said nervously.

'No,' he bit out. 'Would you like to eat out—or are you still unhappy about being seen with me in public?' His voice had hardened.

'James, it isn't that,' she protested. 'You——'

'Then I'll book us a table somewhere, shall I?' he rasped.

'James, I—yes, do that,' she decided firmly.

'Eight o'clock?'

'Yes,' she agreed miserably.

He was still angry with her. And he had a right to be, she acknowledged. Did he really think she was ashamed to be seen in public with him? He would find out just how wrong he was if anyone should recognise her!

'I thought the two of you must have argued.' Her mother sighed her relief when Aura told her she was seeing James that evening.

'Mummy,' she sighed. 'I wish you would understand that James and I are just seeing each other casually. We don't know each other well enough to argue,' she lied.

'If you say so, dear,' her mother accepted vaguely, but this time Aura was *sure* she saw a gleam of laughter in her eyes.

She frowningly watched her mother as she went through to the kitchen with a cat who, if he wasn't already spoilt by the attention that had been lavished on him the last week, was certainly bordering on it, refusing to go back to eating his tinned food, setting up a terrible meowing every evening until he got either boiled fish or chicken for his supper. Well on the way to recovery now, he certainly didn't need the light diet any more, but he was making the most of it, somehow managing to look pitiful if he was denied anything. Her mother denied him nothing.

It was silly to be jealous of a cat, but Aura couldn't help wishing that for once her mother were there for her to talk to, to help her through the trauma of loving James. She wanted someone to pour out her troubles to rather than being the responsible one all the time!

But there was no one; not even Helen was on her side over this, believing that she should tell James the truth and hope he would believe and trust her. Two weeks' acquaintance wasn't long enough to expect him to do that!

The man who called for her that evening was the same one who had been sitting behind that desk on the first day they met, a coldly remote man who hid his feelings behind a mask of impersonal politeness.

'I—had a visitor today.' Finally Aura could stand the silence between them no longer, the restaurant James had chosen quiet and the service unobtrusive, deliberately so, she was sure.

'Oh?' he showed little interest.

He looked so handsome tonight, the black evening suit tailored to him perfectly, his eyes a deep deep green against the darkness of his skin. And he was as approachable as an iceberg!

Aura moistened stiff lips. 'Your partner's wife came to see me.'

Now she had his full attention, his gaze sharp. 'Selina?' he rasped.

'Yes,' she nodded. 'She—invited me to their party on Saturday.'

He sipped the wine the waiter had brought to accompany their meal.

'James, did you hear me?' She knew he had; she

couldn't understand why he didn't show some reaction.

'Yes, I heard you.' He looked at her with narrowed eyes.

'Aren't you interested to know why she came to see me?' Aura snapped.

He shrugged. 'Knowing Selina as I do, what she couldn't achieve one way she decided to achieve another.'

'Which is?' Aura demanded sharply.

'My presence at the party on Saturday,' he decided. 'I refused to go because I knew you wouldn't be interested, and so Selina decided to do a little persuading of her own,' he added drily. 'Are we going?'

She gave a start of surprise. 'Your attendance has nothing to do with me.'

His mouth twisted. 'It has everything to do with you.'

'James, they're your friends,' she protested. 'It's completely your own decision whether or not you attend their party.'

'Even though you know I won't go without you?' He raised dark brows.

'James, did you ask Selina to come and see me?' she frowned.

'Good God, no,' he instantly dismissed. 'I was happy to have an excuse to refuse the invitation.'

'She seems very upset that you aren't going to be there.' Aura picked apathetically at her food.

He shrugged. 'I've attended the last nine,' he drawled. 'And it isn't even compulsory! I'm sorry if Selina's visit upset you but——'

'It didn't upset me,' she said instantly. 'I was a little surprised.' What an understatement! 'But she genuinely seems to want you at their party.'

'That's up to you,' he obstinately reaffirmed.

'Won't it look a little odd if you don't go?' she frowned.

He sighed, suddenly looking very tired. 'To tell you the truth, Aura, I really don't give a damn.' His gaze was pained as it met hers. 'Do you have any idea of the hell I've gone through since we parted on Sunday?' he rasped.

Her breath caught in her throat. 'James . . .?'

'Could we get out of here?' he bit out. 'I'm really not hungry, and you don't seem to be either!'

'I'm not,' she admitted breathlessly.

He settled the bill quickly, the two of them hurrying out to the car, the doors barely closed behind them before they were in each other's arms, mouths fused, hands searching.

'Oh God, I've missed you!' James's forehead rested against hers, their breathing ragged.

'I've missed you too,' she sobbed.

His hands cradled either side of her face as he kissed her slowly, deeply, taking everything she had to give, but giving back with equal measure.

'We're steaming the windows up,' he murmured ruefully some time later.

She gave a choked giggle, her head resting against his chest. 'Like a couple of teenagers!'

His arms tightened about her. 'I don't feel like a teenager. And neither do you,' he drawled self-derisively.

They sat in silence, occasionally kissing, but

mainly just holding each other.

'We can't sit here all night,' Aura finally murmured.

'Ordinarily I wouldn't think of it.' His lips moved against her hair. 'But I'm not about to chance another evening at my apartment when things are still so uncertain between us, and your mother gives us too much privacy at your home too.'

Aura's fingers entangled with the hair on his chest, her hand inside the opening she had unbuttoned at his shirt-front. 'Most men wouldn't complain about that,' she teased.

He was suddenly serious. 'There's no doubting the physical attraction between us; it's the trust that we need to build upon.'

She sighed, regretfully moving out of his arms. 'The real world always has to intrude, doesn't it?'

'I'm afraid so,' he nodded, starting the engine. 'Can I come over tomorrow; I promised your mother a re-match at Scrabble,' he added.

Aura smiled. 'Well if you promised my mother . . I'm sure I can find a friend to visit, or——'

'No good at Scrabble, hm?' he mocked.

Mischief glowed in her eyes, gloriously happy that they seemed to be friends again. 'Wait until tomorrow and see,' she warned.

He clasped her hand as he drove to her home, seeming lost in thought.

But Aura didn't mind, knew that this was nothing like the frosty silence she had known on their drive to the restaurant earlier this evening.

He walked her to her door. 'I won't come in,' he said. 'Give the party on Saturday some thought, will you?' He gently touched her cheek.

She frowned. 'But I thought you didn't want to go?'

'I don't,' he grimaced. 'Unfortunately I don't have a lot of choice. I'd like you to go with me.'

She drew in as ragged breath. 'I don't think I——'

'Aura, tonight I talked about us building up our trust of each other,' he said. 'On the drive here I realised I've been as remiss in that direction as you have.' He sighed at her puzzled expression. 'I don't like going to these damned anniversary parties, they seem the height of hypocrisy to me, but if I don't attend, just once, I know the speculation will start.'

'You mean because Adrian is your partner——'

'I wish that were all it was,' he said disgustedly.

'Then what . . .?

'Most of the guests there—and they're the same year after year——' he rasped, 'know that it should have been *mine* and Selina's anniversary party!'

Aura felt herself pale. 'You mean . . .?'

He drew in a ragged breath. 'Selina was the woman I should have married ten years ago.'

# CHAPTER EIGHT

SELINA MAYHEW? Then that means Adrian was the man she had betrayed James with, the man she had had an affair with and become pregnant by. Robert!

She knew Adrian was capable of taking exactly what he wanted without thought for others, and maybe Jeanne had been right about Selina Mayhew after all. What sort of woman could prefer a shallow bastard like Adrian to someone as wonderful as James?

'She was four years younger than me,' James continued flatly. 'She and Adrian had so much in common. I didn't even see it coming until it was too late. She fainted one evening, and when I called the doctor he said it was just a symptom of her pregnancy, I knew it wasn't my baby, I—I'd never made love to her!'

'Oh, James.' Aura put her arms about him, her cheek resting against his chest. 'How could you bear it?'

'I had no choice,' he rasped. 'Peter, that was Adrian's father,' he explained, 'almost killed Adrian when he found out. Adrian stood in front of the vicar with a black eye,' he recalled grimly.

'How could you bear to have been his partner all these years?' Aura shook her head.

He shrugged. 'It was either that or have everyone

speculate that I must still be in love with Selina—which I'm not,' he added firmly. 'I told you before, I'm not really sure what I felt for her. My parents died when I was twenty-one, and I know I wanted someone of my own to love, a family of my own. Selina was there, beautiful, fun to be with, and when I proposed she accepted. Everything seemed to be working out, until I found out about the baby.'

Adrian and Selina had done this to James. And year after year he had to attend their anniversary party and pretend he was happy for them!

She had disliked Adrian before, but now she totally despised him. And what of Selina Mayhew? Knowing what she did now, she very much doubted the other woman's visit to her today had been as innocent as she pretended it was. Maybe she had just wanted to see exactly what the woman was like who was now seeing James.

'I'll go to the party with you on Saturday,' she decided firmly.

James's expression softened. 'Because you want to or to give me moral support?' he asked. 'If it's the latter I really don't need it,' he smiled. 'I settled this with Adrian years ago, and it isn't even as if the marriage has made either of them happy.'

Aura was more convinced than ever that Selina Mayhew's friendliness today had all been an act, and if there was one thing she couldn't stand it was being made a fool of. Adrian had done it to her once, she wasn't about to let his wife do it too.

'I'm going because I want to,' she told him

determinedly. 'I don't enjoy people assuming I'm stupid!'

James chuckled softly. 'I *know* you aren't,' he murmured. 'Although you might be a little foolish to leave yourself open to Selina's kind of pressure. I've learnt in the last ten years what a lucky escape I had,' he drawled at Aura's surprised look. 'Selina is manipulative, and very determined to have things her own way!'

And no doubt she wanted Aura at her party so that she could attempt to belittle both her and James, believing James wouldn't have told her about their past relationship. Selina Mayhew was in for a surpise if she still believed Aura to be fooled by her friendly act!

As for Adrian, she doubted he would dare object to her presence at his anniversary party, it wasn't very likely that he would announce to his friends that he had tried to get her into his bed!

No, she would go to this party, would stand proudly at James's side and dare anyone to question her right to be there!

'Are you insane?'

She eyed Adrian calmly across the shop, Jeanne at her lunch-break, her only customer having left as Adrian entered.

She had been expecting this visit from him, had known he wouldn't be too pleased about her intention to attend his party with James.

'I don't believe so,' she drawled.

He slammed the door behind him, his face twisted

with anger. 'You *can't* mean to come to the party on Saturday,' he said.

She shrugged. 'How could I refuse when your wife issued such a personal invitation yesterday?'

He became suddenly still. 'Selina came here?'

Aura nodded. 'And stood right where you're standing.'

He gave a guilty start. 'What the hell is she up to now?' he muttered.

'You tell me, she's your wife,' said Aura.

Adrian scowled. 'I thought you didn't want James to know I took you out?'

Aura looked at him coldly. 'Are you going to tell him?'

'No.' He sighed defeatedly. 'Oh, God.' He ran his hand through the thickness of his hair. 'Why the hell did you have to become involved with James?'

'Why did you have to have an affair with his fiancée?' she returned icily.

He looked at her defiantly, a flush darkening his cheeks. 'He told you about that?'

'Yes.' She looked at him with contempt. 'It's called trust, something you and Selina obviously know very little about!'

Adrian sighed again. 'You're making a mistake coming on Saturday.'

Mixing with people she didn't know wasn't something she usually did, always afraid of recognition, but surely there couldn't be any harm in attending a party given for a few friends? She already knew Adrian didn't know the Sutcliffes so there was no chance of her running into any of them there.

'I'm sure it will be a very good party,' she said evenly.

His mouth twisted. 'My wife is renowned for them. She also never stops reminding me that I in no way measure up to James,' he added.

Aura's eyes widened. 'But she married you!'

'What choice did she have?' he bit out. 'It was me or no one; James certainly didn't want her when she was expecting my child.'

Adrian was in love with his wife! Amazing as it might seem, incredible when he constantly had other women in his life—or maybe he had those other women in his life *because* his marriage was such a disaster?—he actually *loved* Selina. And in his wife's eyes he had never matched up to the man she would have married if she hadn't been stupid enough to have an affair with Adrian! What sort of woman *was* Selina Mayhew?

'Lucky James,' she said shakily.

Adrian gave a bitter smile. 'That wasn't what you said the last time we talked about his fiancée's pregnancy!'

'No,' she acknowledged ruefully. 'At least I hope your son doesn't suffer because of the mess you and Selina have made of your lives,' she added harshly.

His expression softened. 'Robert is the one thing we both love.'

She sighed. 'Well, that's something.'

'You won't change your mind about Saturday?' His eyes were narrowed. 'I didn't mean it when I invited you to meet my wife!'

Aura shook her head. 'I've told James I'll go with him.'

Adrian shrugged. 'Well, don't say I didn't warn you.'

He made Saturday night sound very ominous. But at least he was no longer a problem in her life, no longer the threat he had been; she was sure now he wouldn't want to attempt to take the woman James wanted for the second time in his life.

She almost pitied him for the mess he and Selina had made of their lives. Almost. But the pain he had caused James wiped out the emotion.

'I did try to warn you.' James smiled at her bemused expression.

Cars, dozens of them, lined the driveway to the Mayhew house, and even if there were only one person per car—which she very much doubted!—there had to be at least fifty people here. That hardly constituted a 'few friends' in her estimation!

Aura turned to James as he parked his car behind a gold Porsche, hoping her trepidation didn't show. 'Is it always like this?' Her hands were clasped tightly together as she envisaged having to face all these people.

He shrugged. 'Selina looks as if she might have outdone herself this year, but yes, it's usually almost this crowded.'

And for years he had been facing these people alone, she reminded herself firmly. Tonight he wouldn't have to do that—even if she did have to force herself to go in there with him!

She self-consciously checked her appearance as James locked the car, the sun still shining on this mid-June night, picking out the highlights of burnished gold in the deep burgundy of her dress, its knee-length style barely touching on her breasts and hips. Her hair swung loose about her shoulders, a silver-blonde cap that gleamed in the sunshine. Her appearance couldn't be faulted, she realised, only her inner emotions were in turmoil.

James clasped her elbow lightly. 'Just tell me when you've had enough and we'll leave,' he told her drily.

She had had enough! She just hoped the Mayhews didn't know any of the people that mixed socially with the Sutcliffes, and that they weren't invited here tonight. Or, if they were, that Aura Jones remained forgotten by them!

'James!' Selina greeted him warmly, the high-heeled sandals she wore making her almost the same height as he was as she moved to kiss him on the mouth, her hair loose about her shoulders tonight, a slight wave in the ebony sheen, the pure white dress she wore complementing her tan perfectly

Aura looked at the other woman critically tonight, looking for signs of the woman who had humiliated James so badly ten years ago. She still looked the beautifully pleasant woman she had in her shop five days ago!

She turned her attention to Aura. 'I'm so glad you could come after all.' She squeezed Aura's hand.

Aura met James's wry smile, her smile tight as she looked at the other woman. 'Mrs Mayhew,' she returned coolly.

Selina gave one of her throaty laughs. 'I'm sure I asked you to call me Selina,' she said.

'Selina,' she repeated distantly.

The other woman put her arm through the crook of James's. 'We're all friends here, aren't we, darling?' She gazed into James's eyes.

'Yes,' he confirmed drily.

Violet-blue eyes levelled on Aura. 'Aura seems—a little nervous, darling?'

'Aura isn't in the least nervous.' He extricated himself from the clinging woman, his hand once again firm at Aura's elbow. 'She's probably wondering where the champagne is!'

'Of course.' Selina smiled graciously, calling one of the waiters circulating with the bubbly wine to join them. 'A drink can be so soothing, can't it?' she added to no one in particular.

Had that been a barb, a subtle implication that perhaps Aura took a lot of drinks to 'steady her nerves'? The other woman's expression was completely innocent of malice, and yet ... Aura glanced sideways at James as she sensed the slight movement of his body beside her, knowing by the tight control of his mouth that he was *having trouble controlling his mirth*!

She turned back to the other woman. 'Can it?' she returned pointedly.

Selina Mayhew suffered her first loss of composure in Aura's presence, a flush darkening her cheeks. 'I was speaking metaphorically, of course,' she bit out, giving Aura and James a quelling glare.

'Of course.' Aura turned away to take an offered

glass of champagne.

James followed her actions. 'Selina?' he drawled.

'Not just now,' she snapped. 'I still have guests to greet.'

He glanced at the groups of people chatting around the room. 'You mean they aren't all here yet?' His brows rose.

Selina smiled, completely in control once again. 'There are still a few left to arrive, and there are twenty or so people in the garden; it's such a beautiful evening it seems a pity to waste it.' She waved her hand towards the open french doors.

As she did so the flash of diamonds on her wrist caught Aura's gaze, and with a sharply indrawn breath she once again recognised the diamond bracelet Adrian had attempted to give her!

'Lovely, isn't it.' Selina's gaze had followed hers, smiling coyly as she touched the beautiful piece of jewellery. 'It was an anniversary present from Adrian,' she confided lightly. 'I noticed you admiring it when I came to your shop the other day.'

*Admiring* it; she had wished never to see it again! And Adrian had presented it to his wife as an anniversary present. But what else did a man do with a bracelet that had been refused by the woman he was trying to persuade to be his mistress!

'Talking of Adrian,' James drawled, 'where is the lucky man?'

'Probably with one of his golfing cronies discussing the intricacies of the game,' said Selina in a bored voice. 'Take a word of advice from me, Aura,' she grimaced. 'Don't let James take up golf; men become obsessive about it!'

As if she had any say in *what* James did with his life!

But this time she couldn't mistake the other woman's mocking tone and moved closer to James. 'I don't think James has the time, do you—darling?' Her mouth twitched as she met the laughter in his eyes.

His arm moved about her waist. 'Not at the moment, anyway,' he said throatily.

Anger flared in violet eyes before it was quickly masked. 'You shouldn't be *too* possessive with a man, Aura,' she advised softly. 'It makes them feel closed in.'

James's fingers lightly squeezed her waist. 'Aura can close me in any time she wants to,' he drawled.

Selina's composure dropped again, but before she could say anything Adrian joined them, very handsome in his black evening suit and snowy white shirt.

His defiant gaze met Aura's challengingly. 'Miss Jones,' he said drily.

'We've just dispensed with formality, Adrian,' his wife said sharply. 'And don't you think Aura is such a pretty name?'

'Very,' he agreed.

What a strange couple these two made, Aura thought. On the outside they appeared a happily married couple, but they were obviously far from that. And Selina's actions concerning James hinted at jealousy at his being with any other woman. How could the woman be jealous when she had betrayed him with Adrian ten years ago?

Adrian's gaze held Aura's for timeless seconds before he finally turned to his wife. 'Jean and Derek have just arrived,' he said.

'Excuse us,' Selina gave a bright smile before dragging Adrian away with her.

James let out a ragged breath. 'I'll never know why she continues to stay with him.'

Because, as Adrian had said, Selina couldn't have the man she really wanted. It was blazingly obvious, to her at least, and obviously to Adrian to, that Selina Mayhew was still in love with James. If James was aware of it too he chose to ignore it, and Selina, for all her confidence, was afraid of that outright confrontation that might end in rejection. It certainly was a tangled web, but Aura couldn't help feeling grateful for the fact that James had never made the mistake of marrying Selina; she would never have made him happy.

It was hard to imagine James believing himself in love with Selina. He was such a quietly strong man himself, and Selina so dominating, that the marriage would have been certain to be beset by arguments. Or maybe she wasn't being fair to the other woman and perhaps she had only become dominating because she was so unhappy in her marriage.

'Let's go out into the garden,' James suggested with a sigh. 'I could do with some fresh air.'

The balcony outside was crowded too, and they strolled off into the garden, James eager to be away from people. But it had nothing to do with a desire to be alone with Aura, he was lost in thought beside her.

'Are you sure you don't still love her?' She

frowned at his grim expression.

He relaxed with effort. 'I'm sure,' he told her firmly. 'I just—none of this is easy for me, Selina's behaviour, the other guests' curiosity.' He shook his head. 'I hate these damned parties!'

She had noted the curious looks directed at them as they talked with Selina, had hated that interest herself, but for different reasons. 'As soon as it's polite to do so we'll leave,' she promised. 'As you've probably gathered, I hate parties too.'

His arms gathered her into his chest. 'I know you only came for my sake,' he murmured against her hair.

When he held her like this she knew she would do anything for him.

The last week had been a strain, James keeping his distance in a way that made her lie awake in her bed at night aching for him. He spent every evening with her and her mother, was as charming as he had been in the beginning, and he parted from her each night with a searing kiss that left her hungering for more, and more, and more ...

This was the first time they had been alone, completely alone, in five days!

Her mouth moved along his jaw in search of his, and she moaned low in her throat as his parted lips captured hers.

He straightened after all too brief a kiss, ruefully touching her mouth, her lips bare of lip-gloss. 'We had better get back inside, otherwise *we'll* be causing speculation,' he said.

Aura would much rather have stayed out here until

it was time for them to leave, but as everyone seemed so interested in James's reaction to Selina and Adrian she knew they would soon be missed; as it was her slightly less than immaculate appearance was bound to cause talk. Let them talk, she wasn't ashamed to have been in James's arms.

She was laughing softly at something James had said as they went back into the lounge, and was frozen with shock as she looked across the room at Penelope Sutcliffe!

# CHAPTER NINE

SHE had only seen the other woman once before, but it had been a memorable meeting, one Aura would never forget—and she doubted if the other woman had forgotten it either!

The man standing at Penelope's side wasn't Giles Sutcliffe, and Aura looked frantically about the room in case he was here too. She couldn't see him anywhere, but that didn't mean he wasn't here.

Her first instinct was to run, and keep on running, knowing that if that red-haired beauty looked her way just once she would be lost. But what excuse could she give James for their leaving now; they had barely been here half an hour!

She looked back at Penelope Sutcliffe. The other woman hadn't changed in the least during the last two years, she was still as vibrantly lovely as she approached thirty, her red hair a cap of flame about her elfin features, the black gown shimmering about her slender body. And then she turned slightly, and Aura could see that slender line was curved at her stomach; Penelope was very definitely pregnant! A pregnant Penelope was definitely something she couldn't face.

'What is it?'

Aura turned to James as he voiced his concern. 'I—I don't feel very well,' she managed to choke out.

'What's wrong?' He frowned, clasping her arms.

'It's very warm in here, and——'

'You look terrible.' He held her firmly at his side as she swayed. 'I'm taking you home,' he told her determinedly.

'You can't leave,' she gasped in protest. 'What will everyone think?'

His mouth twisted. 'Probably that I can't wait to get you home and into bed!' he derided harshly. 'I don't give a damn what they think; you need to lie down, and——'

'Is everything all right, James?' Selina enquired coolly.

'No, it isn't,' he snapped irritably. 'Aura isn't feeling well; I'm taking her home.'

Selina frowned. 'What's wrong with you?' she asked Aura sharply.

'Nothing! I—a migraine,' she invented. 'They come on so suddenly.' She put up a hand to her temple, all the time aware that the scene they were enacting hadn't yet been observed by Penelope Sutcliffe as she had her back slightly turned towards them. But if she once turned around ...!

'Lie down in one of the spare rooms for a while,' Selina instantly suggested. 'It might pass in a few minutes.'

'No, I—they usually last for hours, sometimes days,' she told them frantically. 'It would really be better if I went home.'

'But——'

'I'm taking her home, Selina,' James cut in firmly. 'Enjoy the rest of your party.' His arm about Aura's waist guided her towards the door.

Aura kept her head down, but as she approached

Penelope Sutcliffe she instinctively looked up.

Maybe if she hadn't done that the green eyes wouldn't have glanced her way, a puzzled frown marring the creamy brow before recognition flared in the now wide green eyes, Penelope's gasp perfectly audible to Aura.

The two women stared at each other for what seemed like an eternity to Aura, but must in fact only have been a couple of seconds, James seeming unaware of the exchange as he steered her determinedly towards the door.

The other woman had recognised her, remembered exactly who she was! Why shouldn't she, she believed Aura was responsible for destroying her family!

Aura, barely aware of saying her goodbyes to Selina and Adrian, breathed deeply of the fresh air once she and James were outside. Her worst nightmare had come true; she had met one of the Sutcliffes and known their hatred once again.

She would have known the nightmare wasn't over if she could have seen Selina's calculating look as Aura went out of the door, turning with a bright smile as she made her way across the room to the woman who had reacted so violently at the sight of Aura Jones.

'I shouldn't have put you through that, I'm sorry,' James told her quietly on the drive home.

The panic was receding a little, and in its place was utter despair. For two years she had avoided such gatherings as Selina Mayhew's party, and the first time, the *very first time* she felt brave enough to face one she had met a member of the Sutcliffe family.

Adrian had told her he didn't know any of the Sutcliffes when she had asked him about them several weeks ago, but as Penelope was pregnant her name was probably no longer Sutcliffe. Did James know the other woman too?

'It wasn't your fault, I've been under a lot of tension lately,' she said wearily.

'Was *that* my fault?' He glanced at her. 'I've been trying to keep things light between us, but the strain is beginning to tell on me too,' he admitted grimly.

'If I asked you to make love to me, would you?'

He drew in a ragged breath. 'No,' he finally answered.

She swallowed hard. 'Why not?'

'You're ill——'

'Not *that* ill,' she chided ruefully.

He sighed. 'I want nothing more than to make love to you. But,' he continued as she would have interrupted him, 'we still don't know each other very well.'

'Is that necessary to make love?' she asked.

'To some men, no. To me, yes.'

She had fallen in love with an honourable man; she couldn't expect him to change now! She smiled weakly. 'I'm sorry I asked.'

'But you didn't.' He shook his head gently. 'You only asked what I would say *if* you did ask.'

She blinked back the tears as she knew he was only saving her pride, that she *had* asked—and been rejected with as much sensitivity as this man always showed her. And he was right, tonight wasn't the right time for them either.

She gave a deep sigh. 'I wish I could have known you years ago!'

'I wish it too,' he smiled.

Her mother had tactfully gone to bed when they got home, and Aura's trembling had subsided enough for her to offer to get them both a cup of coffee.

'I'll get it,' James instantly offered. 'And then you're going straight to bed.'

She smiled wanly. 'I wish that were an indecent proposal!'

He chuckled. 'I'm saving that for when you *really* know me!'

But she did know him, all the important things anyway. She also knew him well enough not to argue with him, knew that he could be as stubborn as she was when he wanted to be.

Ten minutes later her coffee had been drunk, her face gently washed and James was tucking her beneath her bedclothes after ordering her into the bathroom to change into her nightgown.

'Sleep well.' He smoothed back the hair at her temple. 'I'll call you tomorrow.'

'Yes, James,' she returned obediently.

He gave a rueful smile. 'I'm going to kick myself for this when I get home!'

She gave him an inviting smile. 'There's still time to change your mind.'

He sat on the side of her bed. 'When I make love to you—you notice I say when and not if,' he warned, 'we aren't going to do it with your mother in the next room, and we're going to have more than one night to give each other!'

Her brows rose. 'We can only take one night at a time.'

James shook his head. 'Not when there are all the days as well.'

She frowned. 'James, I——'

'Whenever you look like that,' he smoothed the frown from between her eyes, 'I know you're about to warn me about getting involved. I couldn't be more involved if we had been together for years. Think about that tonight.' He tapped her playfully on the nose, kissing her lightly. 'Get your mother to call me if you aren't any better tomorrow, I think I'd enjoy being your nurse!'

But once he had gone Aura could think of nothing but seeing Penelope Sutcliffe again. The other woman might have tried to forget her, her initial puzzlement as she looked at Aura seemed to say she had, but it had only taken that single glance for her to be reminded of all the pain Aura had caused.

She wasn't solely to blame, of course, but she had been the only one left to hate. And hate the Sutcliffes had, with a vengeance that had put Aura's photograph on the front page of several of the more lurid newspapers.

And she had taken it all, all the hatred and accusations, because there had been nothing else she could do. Oh God, let there be no repercussions from her stupidity in believing *she* could ever forget the past and go on with her life.

She had dark lines beneath her eyes the next day, and didn't object when her mother told her to go back to bed and insisted on bringing up a light breakfast for her. It felt wonderful to be coddled by her mother again, and she unashamedly made the most of it, still cuddled up in bed when James arrived mid-morning.

'I've been allocated two minutes by your mother,' he told her ruefully, coming fully into the room to close the door behind him. 'We had better make the most of them!'

She was flush-cheeked and bright-eyed by the time he straightened beside her on the bed. 'Mummy does seem to have taken her duties rather seriously,' she said.

'Still have a migraine?' he asked her.

She shook her head. 'I'm a bit of a fraud really. I didn't sleep very well,' She blushed at the speculative look. 'And when the offer of a lie-in came I took it with both hands. I'm going to get up in a minute.'

'You don't have to worry on my account; I've already invited your mother out on a picnic.' He looked at her teasingly.

Aura smiled. 'And she's refused.'

'No,' he sobered. 'She's still thinking about it.'

Aura became watchful. 'She is?'

James nodded.

'But she hasn't been out since——'

'Ssh,' he chided softly. 'Let's not take any chance of reminding her that she doesn't normally go out.'

Aura couldn't believe her mother was even thinking about leaving the flat, dressing quickly once James had gone back downstairs.

'I have everything in my car for the picnic,' James told her when she joined them. 'Even chilled wine for the ladies and a beer for myself,' he added lightly.

She looked expectantly at her mother, not wanting

to say anything that might tip the scales of her mother refusing to go with them.

James stood up. 'Your coach awaits you, my ladies,' he invited softly.

Still Aura watched her mother, waiting for some move from her. And when it came she held her breath, shaking slightly as her mother gave James a shy smile before allowing him to escort her down to his car.

Tears blinded Aura as she climbed into the back unaided as James settled her mother in the front seat, seeing to her every comfort. Their gazes met in the driving-mirror as he climbed in behind the wheel, and Aura smiled at him gratefully.

James kept up a light conversation that required no answer from the two ladies, covering Aura's shocked silence and her mother's dazed one.

Her mother looked about her curiously, as if everything were suddenly new to her.

'I never knew we had a pond in the park near us, Aura,' she suddenly burst out as they drove past it. 'Perhaps I could come and feed the ducks one day,' she added with childlike enthusiasm.

Aura swallowed hard. 'We always have plenty of dry bread left over,' she encouraged shakily.

'Oh, it's so pretty!' Her mother's eyes glowed. No wonder Marmaduke likes it so much!'

Aura had a feeling the cat's enthusiasm was more for the ducks than the beauty of the park, but she refrained from saying so, although James's conspiratorial smile in the driving-mirror seemed to say that he thought so too!

She couldn't believe her mother had done this, just

walked out of the flat as if she did it every day of her life, instead of having avoided leaving its security as she had for the last two years.

And it was all because of James's influence. He had worked a miracle in their lives, brought freedom to her mother, and love to her. And when he was told about her involvement with the Sutcliffes he was going to hate her, as he despised all deceit. Unless she told him the truth first, as Helen had advised. He was falling in love with her, she was sure he was, and if she couldn't trust the man she loved, whom could she trust!

No opportunity to talk to him alone presented itself that day, the three of them out all day on their picnic and a drive afterwards, and that evening James challenged both women to a game of Scrabble, leaving before her mother went to bed. Aura thought of asking him to stay on a while so that she could talk to him, but tomorrow would be soon enough if it meant that at the end of the day she had lost him. Selina had made a fool of him once; openly to involve himself with Aura would leave him a target for ridicule a second time. Dinner the next night would be plenty of time to lose him if she had to.

The important thing today was that her mother had made a definite step forward, had been interested in the world about her, rather than the indifference Aura had become accustomed to. But a full recovery mustn't be hurried, the doctors had warned her repeatedly, and time was quickly running out for Aura.

'David's late with our delivery of vegetables,' Aura

complained to Jeanne.

'Want me to give him a call?' her assistant offered.

'No, I'll do it,' she replied. 'I enjoy talking to David.' The man who provided their organically grown vegetables for them was a character to say the least.

She had only just finished dialling the number when she heard the shop-bell ring and the sound of Jeanne talking to someone. Someone she recognised all too well!

She forgot the call to David as she hurried out to see Selina Mayhew.

'Aura,' she greeted her with a warm smile. 'You're looking very—bright, today.'

Jeanne caught her eye as the two of them looked down at her dress, the lime green colour definitely 'bright'! But her mood hadn't been all that sunny when she had got up this morning, and the dazzling colour had helped lift her spirits.

'Thank you,' she accepted drily, turning away from Jeanne's knowing look.

Selina looked as beautiful as usual, the pale lemon dress—another designer-label sewn into the back, Aura felt sure—again complementing her deep tan. She had certainly taken advantage of the sunshine in Antigua!

'Did I thank you for the lovely dinner-service you and James gave us on Saturday?' Selina continued lightly. 'It was such a crush, I'm sure I forgot to thank half our guests for their presents.'

'You did thank me,' said Aura, her expression wary, wondering why this woman was really here; it definitely wasn't to express gratitude for presents.

'Although the dinner-service actually came from James.'

Selina's smile seemed to say she had already known that. 'It was lovely, anyway. I'll think of you and James every time I use it.'

Think *what* of her and James? She very much doubted the other woman would get any pleasure from thinking of her doing *anything* with James!

'Actually, I wanted to talk to you about something else.' Selina looked pointedly at Jeanne.

'Don't mind me,' Jeanne drawled drily. 'I have a phone call to make.'

'I'll make the call after Mrs Mayhew and I have talked,' Aura assured her, getting the feeling that what Selina wanted to say to her would be better said in private. 'Would you like to come through to my office, Selina?' she invited. 'Such as it is.'

It was really a small store-room that was too small to store anything of great quantity, the little room only just big enough for two people and her tiny desk near the window.

'What can I do for you, Selina?' she prompted as soon as the door was closed behind them, sitting on the edge of her desk to give them more room.

'Don't you get claustrophobic in here?' Selina asked.

She shrugged. 'I rarely spend enough time in here to do that.' She dusted off the chair that stood behind the desk, bringing it out into the middle of the room. 'Would you like to sit down?' She moved back to the edge of the desk, lacing her fingers together so that the other woman shouldn't see the slight tremble of her hands.

Selina did so gingerly, sitting on the very edge of the chair. Despite the disparity in their positions, Aura being higher than the other woman, it was Selina who was very much in control as she looked at Aura with hard blue eyes.

'I trust you're fully recovered from your migraine?' she bit out.

Aura nodded. 'Fully.'

The violet-blue eyes narrowed. 'I hope none of our guests did—anything, to upset you?'

She stiffened warily. 'I don't believe I spoke to any of them,' she said.

'You seemed perfectly all right when you and James came in from the garden,' Selina said lightly.

'I think it must have been the perfume from the flowers; they can be so heady, can't they?'

'Can they?' the other woman drawled. 'I've never heard of the perfume of flowers bringing on a sudden migraine before.'

'Then perhaps it was something else,' said Aura. 'I'm feeling fine now.'

'You weren't the only one of our guests that had to leave early because she wasn't feeling well,' Selina told her casually.

Aura became rigidly still. 'Oh?'

'No,' the other woman confirmed with a sigh. 'Another friend had to leave just after you because she suddenly felt nauseous.'

Aura drew in a deep breath, her heart pounding in her chest. 'What a pity,' she said lamely, sure she knew exactly which guest it had been.

'I don't know if you know her?' Selina prompted softly. 'Penelope Dalby,' she said. 'She was the only pregnant woman at the party on Saturday night.'

'No, I—I don't believe I know her,' lied Aura.

'No?' Selina arched ebony brows.

'No!'

'Strange,' the other woman drawled. 'She seemed to know you; she went extremely pale when she first caught sight of you.'

She should have known that this woman didn't miss anything that concerned James, and if she had watched the two of them come in from the garden then she had obviously observed her reaction to Penelope Sutcliffe—Dalby, too! Aura waited tensely to hear what else Selina had seen.

Selina stood up, her brows raised as she looked down at Aura. 'But then,' she said slowly, 'I suppose it must be difficult to remain calm when you come face to face with the woman who had an affair with your father!'

# CHAPTER TEN

JEANNE had warned her that this woman would devour her if she got too close, and by accompanying James to the party on Saturday she had definitely been too close!

'You seemed familiar to me the first time I saw you,' Selina continued conversationally. 'But I thought it must be because Adrian always indulges himself with cute little blondes——'

'You know about—about that, too?' Aura gasped.

The other woman looked at her contemptuously. 'Adrian is never subtle,' she said with disgust. 'He thinks that by letting me know about his—little affairs, I'll care enough to be jealous. I never am,' she added with distaste.

Aura swallowed hard. 'Adrian told you he had—he had taken me out a few times?'

'He never *tells* me, Aura,' the other woman dismissed tauntingly. 'He leaves receipts for flowers—and jewellery, lying about for me to "accidentally" find,' she drawled in a bored voice.

The flowers he had sent her. And the bracelet! My God, the bracelet ... She stared at it as it gleamed brightly on the other woman's slender wrist.

'Yes, *this* jewellery,' Selina held her wrist up mockingly. 'Such a pretty bauble. Why on earth did you refuse it, Aura?' she derided. 'If you didn't like it you could always have sold it. I would have thought a woman like you would be aware of the fact that it's worth several thousand pounds.'

'A woman like you . . .' She had no doubt what this woman believed her to be!

'Adrian and I only ever went out to dinner together,' she said stiffly. 'At the time I had no idea he was married and had a child.'

'Would it have made any difference if you had known?' Selina scorned.

'Yes!' she rasped. 'No matter what you've heard, I am not a home-wrecker!'

'Nigel Sutcliffe died in your bed, my dear,' the other woman drawled. 'He had a wife and two children; I would class that as home-wrecking!' she derided.

Aura felt faint, closing her eyes to stop the room swaying precariously. What could she say in answer to the truth!

'Such a scandal,' Selina tutted. 'The Sutcliffes are socially one of the most prominent families in the country. And the head of that family died in *your* bed!' She laughed softly. 'It took me a while to put all the pieces together, your migraine at the sight of Penelope, her sudden attack of nausea for the same reason, seeing you. Penelope wouldn't tell me anything, denied ever seeing you before, but I wasn't fooled for a moment.'

Aura's eyes blazed. 'You *knew* there was some dirt you could dig up somewhere!'

'My dear,' the other woman chided. 'The truth has a way of being heard.'

She drew in as ragged breath. 'Why have you told me all this? What do you want from me?'

Selina's mouth twisted. 'Oh, I think you know the answer to that.'

She wanted her out of James's life! Wanted her as far away from him as possible. Because although she posed no threat to Selina's marriage, the other woman not caring enough about Adrian to give a damn about his affairs, she wasn't about to let her remain in James's life, possibly to have him fall in love with her!

'Just your having been out with Adrian might have been enough to shake James,' Selina told her lightly. 'But there's no guarantee that between the two of you you couldn't convince him it was all perfectly innocent between you two. Not that I believe it was,' she added harshly. 'But I'm sure Adrian wants James angry with him no more than you do.'

'It *was* all perfectly innocent between us,' Aura insisted tightly.

'Do you really think I care one way or the other?' the other woman scorned. 'Adrian's little affairs ceased to interest me a long time ago. As I'm sure they did James. But there's no way *you* can explain away the death of your lover in your bed!' she added with satisfaction. 'I remember the newspapers were full of it at the time. It isn't surprising the poor man expired,' she mocked. 'A fifty-two-year-old man trying to keep up with the demands of a twenty-two-year-old woman!'

'Don't be disgusting!' Aura snapped, her hands clenched into fists.

Dark brows rose. '*I* wasn't the one that was disgusting, Aura,' Selina drawled.

Her mouth was tight. 'If you think James would be so interested in this, why don't you go and tell him?' she challenged.

Selina gave a malicious smile. 'I thought I would leave that to you.'

Aura gasped. 'You expect me——'

'I expect *you*,' the other woman cut in firmly, 'to tell James you can't see him any more. No more need be said about this—other business, if you do that.'

Her eyes widened. 'I would have thought you would *enjoy* telling him about me!'

'James is a very proud man,' Selina bit out coldly. 'He is hardly likely to turn to me for comfort if I were the one to tell him what a fool he's been.'

'Especially as you did so much worse to him ten years ago!' Aura glared. 'What on earth makes you think James would turn to *you* in any circumstances?' she scorned.

Selina looked at her with dislike. 'James has never stopped caring for me,' she told her scornfully. 'It's only his pride that's stood in our way.'

Aura's one consolation in having to tell James the truth was that, no matter what the outcome of their conversation, she knew he would never turn to this woman for anything!

Selina watched her fleeting expression of satisfaction with narrowed eyes. 'I'd rather not do it,' she told her softly. 'But, believe me, if it becomes necessary, I *will* tell James about you!'

'I'll talk to him,' rasped Aura. 'But I wouldn't start

making any long-term plans for the two of you!'

The other woman gave a disbelieving laugh. 'You don't seriously expect him to stay with you if I have to tell him about your deceased lover, do you?'

'I don't *seriously* expect him to turn to you if there were only the two of you left on earth!' Aura told her derisively.

Selina's mouth tightened in an ugly sneer. 'He was once going to marry me; I doubt he's offered you anything more than a few hours in his bed!'

Aura met her bitter gaze calmly. 'I thought we had just agreed that's something I'm very good at.'

'We'll see who's laughing by this time tomorrow!' the other woman challenged.

'Oh, I get twenty-four hours to tell James, do I?' she derided. 'That means I needn't tell him until the morning,' she added pointedly, wishing this woman gone, wishing she could curl up in a foetal ball and forget the world existed.

Angry colour darkened the other woman's cheeks. 'You'll tell him tonight,' she rasped. 'Because if you don't he'll get a visit from me tomorrow!'

Aura was shaking so badly by the time the other woman left that she sat trembling on the edge of her desk for several minutes after she had gone.

Selina knew, not just about Adrian, although God knows that was bad enough, but about that other scandal, the death of Nigel Sutcliffe in her bed that had made her run from all that was familiar to her, hiding behind the façade of London's anonymity.

Was she going to have to run again? Where could she go that the past didn't find her?

She could have wept for Penelope Dalby on
Saturday, knew how hurt the other woman had been
when she heard how her father had died. Thank God
Penelope's brother Giles hadn't been at the party
too; Giles had been very vocal, to Aura and the press,
about his opinion of the little gold-digger who had
tricked his father into an affair. If they had met on
Saturday he would no doubt have loudly repeated his
disgust for all the other guests to hear.

Aura could understand their pain, knew how
deeply they had loved and respected their father. And
she could understand his wife's bitterness. What
none of them seemed to have understood was that she
had loved him too ...

'Are you all right?' Jeanne looked at her worriedly.

She straightened, giving a wry smile. 'I think the
Venus Flytrap just went into action,' she revealed
wanly. 'Although I think I resent being a fly!' she
added in an attempt at lightness.

Jeanne sighed. 'I thought she looked pretty smug
when she went out of here,' she said disgustedly.
'You——' she broke off as the telephone rang.
'Maybe that's David to explain why he hasn't
delivered the vegetables yet,' she grimaced.

Aura was relieved to have to deal with such a
mundane task, although she nearly dropped the
receiver when the woman on the other end of the line
identified herself. Penelope Dalby!

'Miss Jones?' she prompted as she received only
silence after the announcement. 'Aura?' she said
again quietly.

Aura's palm was so wet with perspiration she was

in danger of dropping the receiver. 'I'm sorry,' she finally managed to choke out, 'there's no one of that name here.'

'Aura, I want to talk to you,' said the other woman.

So that she could throw out more accusations? She had had enough for one day! 'I told you there's no one of that name here,' she snapped, evading Jeanne's puzzled gaze. 'You must have the wrong number!'

'No, I——'

'I'm sorry,' Aura said again before slamming the receiver back down on its cradle, staring at it as if it were a viper about to strike. When it instantly began ringing again she backed away from the desk. 'Jeanne, I—— There's someone on the end of that line I don't want to talk to.' She looked up with frantic eyes. 'Could you tell her that Aura Jones isn't here?'

'Of course.' Jeanne didn't question her desperation, picking up the receiver. 'I understand, Mrs Dalby, but I'm afraid we have no Miss Jones here,' she answered patiently. 'No, I'm not the woman you were talking to a moment ago,' she acknowledged softly. 'No, that wasn't Miss Jones either. I'm sorry, Mrs Dalby, I think you must have the wrong number,' she added firmly before ringing off. She turned to Aura. 'I don't think she's going to give up,' she said regretfully.

Couldn't the Sutcliffes leave her alone? Hadn't they done enough to her in the past?

'Jeanne, I'm going out for the rest of the day,' she decided. 'Can you manage on your own?'

'Of course,' her assistant answered. 'Are you going to be all right?' she frowned.

'Probably not,' she grimaced. 'I need to be on my own for a while, to think. I have some working out to do.'

'What shall I tell Mr Ballantine if he calls?'

It was what *she* was going to tell James that she had to think about! 'He shouldn't call.' She shook her head. 'We're meeting later tonight. But if he does——' She chewed on her bottom lip. 'Just tell him I'll see him later.' She shrugged uncertainly.

She drove to the spot that had been her secret place as a child, the spot she always went to when she needed to be alone, to dream, to think, or just to admire the beauty of the countryside surrounding the hill she sat up on the top of.

The small village of Stadford nestled just behind her, and in front of her were rolling hills and patchwork fields as far as the eye could see, cows munching happily on grass, crops growing in the remaining fields.

This had been the home of her childhood, uncomplicated, with every new adventure exciting. And even when she had stopped being a child, life had still seemed full of possibilities—not quite as untarnished as she had always dreamt, but full of challenge nonetheless. Until the night Nigel Sutcliffe died in her arms.

A nightmare couldn't begin to describe that night, the pain of loss, the sudden glare of publicity that had surrounded her once the press learnt where the rich industrialist had died. She had run, hidden from her accusers, but now, today, she had to face them all over again, had to tell the man she loved of the horror of that night.

She was going to tell him all of it, and hoped he loved her enough to understand. She had no other choice!

She was tired but resigned when she returned to the shop later that afternoon, had spent the whole day sitting on top of that hill, the simplicity of her surroundings giving her the strength to face James.

Jeanne had locked up for the night, had just finished doing the books. She looked up as Aura quietly let herself into the office. What she saw in Aura's face seemed to reassure her.

'Mr Ballantine did call,' she told her briskly. 'Just to remind you he'll pick you up at eight.'

'Thanks,' she nodded.

Jeanne sighed, clearing away. 'That Mrs Dalby called three more times after you left. Each time I told her there was no Aura Jones here. The last time she asked me to give the non-existent Miss Jones her telephone number. It's on the pad over there.' She pointed in the direction of the telephone.

Aura didn't even glance towards it. 'Thanks, Jeanne. You get along home now,' she said.

She locked up after her assistant, turned off the lights, and went upstairs, all without looking at the notepad containing Penelope Dalby's telephone number.

Her mother was in her usual spot in front of the television, watching a children's programme if the childlike laughter on the sound-track was anything to go by. Almost as if yesterday had never happened. And maybe it hadn't. One picnic didn't mean her mother would ever be normal.

She got her mother's dinner and cleared away, fed the completely recovered cat, and then went up to change before James arrived.

She had no idea how to approach the subject of a man dying in her bed! How could she even introduce such a thing into the conversation, she thought hysterically.

'You're very quiet.' James frowned at her once they were out in the car.

'A long day,' she shrugged, wondering why he didn't start the engine so that they could get on with this.

'Where were you when I called?'

'I had to go out,' she evaded. 'James,' she drew in a deep breath. 'Would you mind if we didn't go out to dinner tonight?'

His brows rose. 'Another migraine?'

She sighed, knowing what he was thinking. 'No. I—I need to talk to you. I'd rather do that at your apartment.' She looked at him pleadingly.

'If that's what you want,' he shrugged, sitting back to switch on the ignition. 'You seem very— troubled.' He spoke again once they had been travelling for several minutes. 'You aren't about to tell me you can't see me again, are you?'

There was no teasing in his voice, as if he guessed this wasn't a time for that. 'There are some things I have to tell you,' was her only answer.

His mouth tightened. 'Sounds ominous.'

It sounded like a death-knell to her! Was James going to understand, about Adrian, about Nigel Sutcliffe? Would any man understand!

He poured them both a drink once they were in his apartment, a brandy for each of them, as if he knew they were going to need it.

'So—tell me,' he invited, his eyes narrowed as she sat stiffly on the sofa.

She sipped the brandy, instantly warmed by the unaccustomed alcohol. Start with the lesser of two evils, she told herself firmly. 'That first day when I came to your office,' she took another sip of the brandy, 'I told you that I had dealt with Adrian in the past.'

James leant against the fireplace. 'Yes.'

'We—met some weeks before.' She stared down into her glass rather than at James, not wanting to see the dawning of disgust in his eyes. 'We went out together several times,' she added in a rush. When there was no audible reaction she looked up sharply, searching his face for accusation, finding him staring back at her almost questioningly. 'Did you hear me, James?' she prompted harshly. 'I said I went out with Adrian several times!'

He nodded slowly. 'And?'

'And?' she repeated shrilly. 'And I went out with your partner, your *married* partner!'

James shrugged. 'You didn't know he was married.'

'How——' She gaped at him. 'James, why are you taking this so calmly?' She shook her head in disbelief.

'Because I already knew about it,' he told her softly.

She swallowed hard. 'You couldn't have done,' she shook her head again. 'You wouldn't have gone out with a woman who had been involved with Adrian.'

'You're right,' James nodded. 'I wouldn't. But you weren't involved with him.'

'How—how did you know that?' she stared at him.

'I told you that first day I would look into the mistake concerning your lease. Only when I looked into it I found there had been no mistake, that Adrian had left strict instructions for your lease not to be renewed—at least until he came back from his holiday. It didn't take a genius to work out that you had been the latest woman in his life, or to realise that things hadn't gone as he wanted them to.' He shrugged. 'I knew for certain when I saw you that night and mentioned that my partner had taken his wife away on holiday. You went very white; for a moment I thought you were going to faint. Good God, Aura, I don't usually reveal the private life of my partner to complete strangers,' he added harshly as she still looked disbelieving. 'I told you the truth about Adrian to let you know exactly what a bastard you had turned down!'

He knew. All this time he had known the truth about her and Adrian!

'I waited for you to tell me, Aura,' he sighed. 'I left the way open several times for you to do so. When you didn't I decided the incident must be too painful for you, that learning that Adrian was married with a child had deeply shocked you.'

'It did,' she confirmed shakily.

'You aren't to blame for Adrian's infidelity,' he said. 'He lied and cheated with you, just as he's lied and cheated all his life!'

Aura stared at him as if she had never seen him before. 'You really don't blame me?'

'No,' James bit out grimly. 'You were so angry that day in my office, as if you knew you had much more than a clerical error to deal with. I can't say I was surprised when I learnt of Adrian's part in all this.'

'But you were—disappointed?' she prompted tensely.

'In you?' He shook his head. 'I knew you must have turned him down for Adrian to be so vindictive. And I was already starting to fall in love with you,' he added softly.

Aura looked at him sharply, at last able to see the love in his face that she had been afraid to acknowledge. Would that love still be there once she had told him everything?

'I've had just about all I can take of Adrian,' James continued harshly. 'The partnership is in the process of being dissolved.'

'Because of me?' she gasped.

'Not completely,' he said. 'I continued the partnership originally because of Adrian's father, Peter. And also because I just couldn't be bothered to go through all the speculation there would have been if I hadn't,' he admitted with a sigh. 'But learning what Adrian tried to do to you, the intimidation to get what he wanted, made me wonder if he had done the same thing with other women he decided he wanted. That dishonesty is something I *can't* accept from my business partner; my lawyers are working out the details for the split now.'

She was glad, because James was too honourable a man to be classed with a man like Adrian!

But Adrian had only been the first of her confessions!

'James,' she began slowly. 'There's a very good reason why I—I shied away from a man who tried to buy me!' She looked at him anxiously.

His eyes narrowed. 'The man that hurt you in the past?'

'Yes,' she acknowledged dully. 'I—there was once another man in my life who had a wife and children he couldn't leave!' Her head went back in challenge, her breathing ragged as she defiantly met his gaze.

There was new tension about him now. 'Did you love him?' he finally asked.

'Yes.'

'Did he love you?'

'Very much,' she said without hesitation.

'And he tried to buy you?' he prompted softly.

She drew in a ragged breath. 'He—was very rich.'

'But did he try to buy you?' James persisted.

'He—bought me things,' she bit out. 'Lots of things.'

'What happened to him?' James rasped.

She closed her eyes, shaking badly by the time she opened them again. 'He died.'

James looked as if she had hit him. 'And if he—

hadn't died,' he spoke quietly, 'he would still be in your life now?'

Undoubtedly. There would be no question of it. 'Yes,' she admitted huskily.

'I'm in love with you, you know that,' he told her gruffly.

She quickly averted her face so that she didn't have to see the pain in his eyes. 'I only wanted to be with you for a while, to be allowed to love you,' she choked.

She heard him move, and suddenly he was down on his haunches in front of her, gently wiping away the tears. 'What happened to change that?' His complete vulnerability was clear in his eyes.

'Selina.'

His expression sharpened, fury glittering in his eyes now. 'She found out about this and threatened you?' he ground out.

Aura sighed shakily. 'She's still in love with you. She's afraid you'll fall in love with me.'

'She's already too late to stop that,' he bit out grimly. 'My God, she and Adrian surely deserve each other! But it doesn't matter, Aura,' he dismissed impatiently. 'You've told me now, we love each other——'

'There's more,' she cut in softly. 'Much more. You've survived one scandal, but this one is much worse than that. We can never have more than we have right now!' She looked at him imploringly.

'Allow me to be the judge of that,' he rasped.

'He—Nigel, was at my apartment when he died,' she told him in a rush. 'In my bed.'

Only the darkening of his eyes told her she had hurt him more. 'So he died in your bed——'

'James,' she cut in shrilly. 'His name was Sutcliffe, Nigel Sutcliffe!'

His eyes widened with shock. 'But he was——'

'One of the best known businessmen in England,' she finished. 'Possibly *the* best known. His family was worth millions, always have been.'

James straightened, looking down at her disbelievingly, shaking his head, as if he *couldn't* believe it. 'I remember the scandal,' he said distractedly, 'the publicity. But I didn't read much about it because I abhor that sort of sensationalism.'

'If you *had* read about it you would have learnt that Nigel Sutcliffe often visited my apartment, that the night he died he had a heart attack there,' she revealed dully. 'The press hounded me, wouldn't leave me alone, wanted our exclusive story,' she said disgustedly.

James didn't answer, and she looked up at him sharply, finding him deep in thought. What was he thinking, what was he going to say when she told him the rest of it?

'It wouldn't be fair for me to expect you to involve yourself with a woman connected with such a scandal,' she said softly. 'Selina remembered me, and there would ultimately be others. I wouldn't want to drag you down with me. You're *my* secret passion.'

'This is why you've been trying to stop seeing me,' he said. 'Even though it wasn't what you really wanted. Was it?' He looked at her intently.

'I love you,' she told him shakily.

He pulled her to her feet. 'And I love you, have waited a lifetime for you. I'm not about to lose you now,' he added arrogantly, burying his face in her hair. 'If we have to we'll face this together, Aura.'

'I can't do that to you! I'll refuse to see you again,' she added desperately.

He drew back to smile. 'Darling, you can't stop me loving you. And if you won't see me I'll just have to camp on your doorstep, and if I do that it's sure to draw attention to us,' he warned.

'A married man died in my flat——'

'Yes,' James cut in softly. 'But he was your father. Wasn't he?'

# CHAPTER ELEVEN

AURA swallowed hard, staring up at James as if she couldn't believe what he had just said. And she couldn't!

How had he known? How had he guessed that Nigel Sutclife had been her mother's lover, not her own? No one else had realised that two years ago.

'Wasn't he?' James said again, shaking her slightly.

'Where on earth did you get that ridiculous idea?' she dismissed brittly. If James wouldn't walk away from the scandal being involved with her would bring to him then she was going to have to *force* him away from her. And telling him the truth was now out of the question!

'Just now,' he said quietly, 'when you told me the name of the man who died you presumed I was about to show surprise at his identitiy. I wasn't. I was about to say he was old enough to be your father.' He shook his head. 'I've come to know you very well, Aura, and involving yourself with a married man is not something I believe you would do. There had to be another explanation for his being at your flat that night. A father is entitled to vist his daughter,' he shrugged.

Aura pulled away from him. 'You don't believe I'm capable of having an affair with a married man but you believe my mother *is*?' she scorned.

'I believe,' he said softly, 'that your mother fell deeply, and irrevocably, in love with a man who couldn't leave his wife.'

'Couldn't?' Aura challenged.

'Elizabeth Sutcliffe has been in a wheelchair since she was involved in an accident just after her second child was born. What kind of bastard would her husband have looked if he had asked her for a divorce after that?' James frowned.

'He——'

'Aura, it would be quite a simple thing to check who your father was,' he put in quietly.

She was trembling so badly she had to sit down, falling weakly into the chair behind her. James was right, it *would* be a simple thing to check the identity of her father, and it said very clearly on her birth certifcate that his name was Nigel Sutcliffe!

'It wasn't just because his wife was an invalid,' she said flatly. 'He loved my mother enough to withstand the scandal leaving his wife would have caused. But he refused to drag my mother through the scandal his wife threatened to bring about them if he should attempt to divorce her.' Aura looked up at James with tears in her eyes. 'I feel so sorry for her, know how awful it must be to be confined to a wheelchair. But I hate her too, because my mother and father loved each other very much, and they were never able to declare that love openly!'

James pulled her to her feet, taking her place in the chair, before settling her on his lap. 'Tell me about it,' he urged gently.

It wasn't easy to talk about her unorthodox childhood, the father who spent weekends with them, but Monday to Friday with his 'other' family, she learnt when she was old enough to realise her father's behaviour was different from that of other fathers. Her mother could have lied, could have told her he had a job that took him away from them during the week, but she hadn't done that, had openly told her daughter of the love-triangle that had claimed them.

Nigel Sutcliffe had been living with his wife, but separately, for over three years when he met Aura's mother. She had been his temporary secretary, and from that brief meeting had come a love so strong that, although they had both fought against it, and had deliberately not seen each other for six months, it just wouldn't be denied.

Nigel had tried to do the honourable thing, had asked his wife for a divorce, genuinely believing that they would both be happier apart. His wife had flatly refused, had threatened to expose Aura's mother for the home-wrecker that she was.

Again her mother and father had tried to stay away from each other, but they had loved so deeply that they just couldn't do it. When Aura's mother became pregnant with her Nigel had again asked his wife for a divorce, but this time she had warned him that if he asked again she was going to go to the press about his little affair, to make sure that everyone knew about the woman who had stolen the husband of a woman confined to a wheelchair. Nigel refused to have his beloved Meg slandered in that way, especially as once his wife found out about their expected baby she would denounce that as a bastard too.

Aura pressed her face against James's chest. 'They

never did marry, but they loved each other more than any other couple I've ever seen.'

'And you lied two years ago to protect your mother,' he guessed.

'I didn't lie,' she said. 'No one ever asked me if Nigel Sutcliffe was my lover, they all just assumed that he was.' She drew in a ragged breath. 'Mummy was with him that night, they had both been over for dinner. When he—when he collapsed, we managed to get him on to my bed, and Mummy sat with him while I called a doctor. By the time I got back to the bedroom I could see it was too late, and we—we both held him until he just stopped breathing.' Tears fell unheeded down her cheeks. 'Mummy went into shock, and—and she's never come out of it. I couldn't let those people ask her the questions they asked me.' She shuddered. 'Perhaps they shouldn't have fallen in love, and they should certainly never have had me, but Elizabeth Sutcliffe made us all pay for the fact that she wasn't prepared to relinquish her role as Mrs Nigel Sutcliffe even though she hadn't loved her husband for years! Love isn't about owning or possessing, it's about just wanting to be together.'

'The way we want to be together,' James put in softly.

She looked up at him. 'I decided in the end not to tell you the truth because it would have been easier to let you believe Nigel Sutcliffe really had been my lover, but even now that you do know the truth it makes no difference to us.'

'I agree,' he drawled. 'And *not* telling me the truth wouldn't have either. You see, I would have known the moment I made love to you.'

'James, haven't you heard a word I've just said?' She sat up. 'I can't be involved with you——'

'Loving me isn't being involved?' he mocked.

She gave a shaky sigh. 'I will not expose you to the lies the press will print about me if they ever find out we love each other!'

'It wouldn't bother me in the slightest,' he dismissed. 'I don't give a damn about their lies. But if it bothers *you* we can have a quiet wedding——'

'Wedding?' she spluttered. 'I'm not going to marry you!'

'Of course you are——'

'No!'

He stood up with her still in his arms. 'I insist on being your husband as well as your lover,' he smiled.

'But we haven't—I mean, we aren't——'

'No,' he acknowledged softly. 'But we're about to!'

Her cheeks were fiery-red as he carried her through to his bedroom, placing her gently down on the bed. 'James, let me out of here——'

'No,' he told her firmly. 'I don't intend to release you until you admit you belong to me and agree to marry me.' He threw off his jacket and began to unbutton his shirt.

She should be running for the door, should make her escape before it was too late, but she lay weakly back on the bed, watching his every movement, marvelling at the beauty of his body as he stood completely naked before her.

Her clothes were removed with the same unhurried care, and as the lean length of his body lay beside hers she gave herself up to the magic of his touch.

Languor gave way to passion, deep and all-consuming, their kisses fevered, their caresses heated, each of them desperate to imprint the image of sight and touch in their memory for ever.

When James gently joined his body with hers, Aura knew she was at last whole, that she had found the other half of herself, and she met his driving need with a fire of her own, both of them consumed in the flames as the pleasure devoured them.

James held her against him, caressing her hair with soothing motions as the quakes still shook her body. 'How could a virgin have had an affair with *any* man?' he lightly chided her.

She buried her face against his damp chest, her fingers entwined with the curling tendrils of hair there. 'I love you the way my parents loved each other. But——'

'No buts,' he cut in firmly, his arms tightening about her. 'We're going to be married as soon as I can arrange it. And then I'm going to take care of you and your mother for the rest of our lives.'

'You love her too,' Aura realised softly.

'As a son,' he nodded. 'There's something about your mother that cries out for a man to protect her. I can understand why your father didn't want her hurt by the cruelty of what the world would make of their love and the child it had created. You have that same vulnerability, although caring for your mother has made you put up a veneer to protect yourself. From now on I'm going to take care of both of you,' he told her determinedly.

'I don't want you hurt.'

'I don't think I could survive the pain if I lost *you*,' he told her gruffly.

She gave a shaky smile. 'Even if we did manage to avoid meeting anyone who might recognise me, even if you did manage to persuade me to marry you, Selina isn't going to give up.'

'We aren't going to hide from anyone—although to give *you* peace of mind we won't flaunt our marriage either,' he conceded at her panicked look. 'We *are* getting married. And you can leave Selina to me,' he finished grimly.

The idea of letting James take control, of relinquishing the worry and fear of the past to him, was a good one. But was it fair?

He looked down at her with love-filled eyes. 'Do you love me?' he prompted.

'Oh yes. But——'

'I told you, no buts. We love each other, that's enough.'

She wasn't so sure of that when they returned home to tell her mother the good news and found Penelope Dalby sitting in the lounge with her!

Aura could feel herself pale, looking anxiously at her mother, her tranquil expression reassuring her before she turned accusingly to Penelope Dalby.

James took one look at her face and turned to her mother. 'Shall we go and make some coffee, Meg?' he prompted lightly.

Her mother stood up. 'Mrs Dalby said it was urgent she talk to you, Aura,' she told her lightly. 'I didn't think you would mind if she waited.'

'No—it's fine.' She gave a shaky smile. 'Mrs Dalby and I have some—unfinished business to discuss.' She waited only long enough for James to escort her mother into the kitchen before turning on the other woman. 'How dare you come here?' she glared.

Penelope Dalby's head went back proudly, only the pulse at her throat telling of her own nervousness. 'I wanted to meet the woman my father loved,' she said challengingly.

Aura stiffened. 'Surely my refusal to take your calls today must have told you that I don't share your curiosity!'

'I also wanted to meet my sister.'

Aura blinked, feeling herself sway, regaining control with effort. 'What did you say?' she finally gasped.

'Oh, Aura.' The other woman sat forward, her advanced pregnancy making her clumsy. 'I know you're my sister, that it was your mother our father loved.'

She swallowed hard, moistening dry lips. 'How?'

Penelope sighed. 'My mother was very bitter after Daddy died; don't ask me why, she hadn't loved him for years,' she grimaced. 'She actually seemed glad that he had died the way he did, enjoyed the way you were blackened in the newspapers. Giles was very upset about it too——'

'I know that,' she snapped.

The other woman gave a rueful smile. 'Giles has always had a temper. But once he calms down he can be quite astute. And you bear a striking resemblance to Grandmother Sutcliffe.'

'I do?' she said uncertainly, never having known a grandparent's love, her mother's parents already dead by the time Aura was born. It was a little strange to find out you looked like someone you had never met—and were never likely to meet, she reminded herself firmly!

'Mm,' Penelope noded. 'Giles did some checking up. Was he angry when he found out the truth!' she sighed. 'I've never seen my brother—our brother, that furious before.'

'I can understand him being upset about my mother and your father——'

'Oh he wasn't upset about that,' the other woman said. 'He was angry with our mother for holding on to her marriage by threatening Daddy with never seeing his two children again if he divorced her!'

'She—did—that—too?' Aura trembled at the bitterness of the woman.

Penelope nodded. 'As far as we can make out, Mummy threatened everyone involved so that she could hang on to a marriage that had been dead for years. Giles was all for finding you and exposing the pack of lies the press had been given, but Grandmother—the one you look like,' she added gently, 'seemed to think that we had hurt you and your mother enough already.' She turned in the direction of the kitchen. 'Has she been that way since Daddy died?' There was a catch in her voice.

'Yes.' Aura didn't pretend not to understand. 'She's blocked out his death because it's too painful for her to comprehend. And yet he died in our arms.'

'I'm glad he was with people who loved him.' Her half-sister gave a tremulous smile. 'My mother is very ill, in fact I don't expect her to live to see her first grandchild——'

'I'm sorry.' The impulsive exclamation was instinctive.

Penelope shook her head. 'She hasn't lived a happy life—by her own choosing,' she added sadly. 'I want——' she began again. 'I want my baby to know its aunt.' She looked beseechingly at Aura. 'You have a brother and a grandmother who want to know you to. I couldn't believe it when I saw you at the Mayhews' party the other evening.' Her eyes glowed. 'But before I could say anything you had left.'

'With the man I intend to marry.' Aura said.

Again Penelope glanced towards the kitchen. 'He seems very nice.'

'He is,' she confirmed. 'He also knows about my mother and your father.'

'Our father,' the other woman reminded pointedly.

She drew in a ragged breath. 'You've seen my mother; she isn't even aware that he's dead, let alone up to my suddenly being acknowledged as a Sutcliffe!'

Hazel eyes filled with tears. 'Giles and I want to know our sister. My grandmother is anxious to meet you too——'

'You've told her you've seen me again?' Aura gasped.

'Yes,' Penelope nodded. 'Haven't enough people already suffered because two people fell in love?'

'One of them was a married man!'

'He didn't want to be,' her sister reminded her gently.

'I can't become involved with you,' Aura denied brokenly. 'Not if it means endangering the little stability my mother has found.'

'She's very beautiful.' Penelope sighed. 'Can you ever forgive us?'

Aura drew in a harsh breath. 'You were as innocent as I was!'

The other woman shook her head. 'We made things worse for you after Daddy died.'

'It doesn't matter now,' said Aura, realising that James couldn't delay her mother in the kitchen for ever. 'I'm glad you came to see me tonight—I couldn't imagine what you wanted to talk to me about——'

'I'm sure you imagined I wanted to hurt you again,' Penelope said ruefully, standing up with an effort. 'I'll let you know if you have a nephew or niece,' she added gently.

A sister and a brother who wanted to know her, plus a grandmother who would like to meet her; but it couldn't be! After years of being denied by the Sutcliffes it was difficult to give up the family she had never been allowed to know.

But she did it.

# CHAPTER TWELVE

WERE all brides this nervous, she wondered? She had been awake since six o'clock, unable to get back to sleep, even though the wedding wasn't until three o'clock in the afternoon.

The last month had been a rush, James insisting they had a church wedding, even if they were having only half a dozen guests present.

Two weeks ago Aura had seen the announcement of the death of Elizabeth Sutcliffe, and although it had been this woman's vindictiveness that caused so much unhappiness her heart had gone out to Penelope and Giles; no matter what else Elizabeth Sutcliffe had been, she was still their mother.

James hadn't altogether approved of her decision not to see her brother or sister, but he couldn't see any way around hurting her mother either, and so Aura had sent only a note of condolence on the death of Penelope's and Giles's mother. She had received a small note back from Penelope thanking her for her kindness. It had been the only contact between the two sisters.

James's partnership with Adrian was well on the way to being dissolved, and by the time they returned from their honeymoon the final papers should be ready for signing.

Cocooned by James, she had no idea what he had

said to Selina Mayhew, but the woman hadn't bothered her again.

'Are you sure you want Jonathan for your pageboy?' Helen was struggling to get the tiny bow-tie on the wriggling child.

'I'm sure,' she smiled. 'And Annie looks adorable in her dress.' She smiled at her little bridesmaid.

Helen shook her head, looking decidedly harassed. 'They'll probably start fighting half-way down the aisle!'

Aura smiled again; nothing could daunt her today. It was the happiest day of her life; the day of her marriage to James.

They fitted into each other's lives perfectly, James introducing her to several of his close friends, people whom she liked and who liked her, all of them accepting her without question. And James's liking for Helen and Simon had increased, knowing they had been her staunchest supporters throughout the trauma of the last two years, that, as a childhood friend, Helen knew the whole story.

The Collisters, her mother, a friend of James's who was standing as best man, two other couples he had felt close enough to invite, Jeanne and her family, were the only guests. Aura didn't care if they had no guests at all, as long as she was James's wife at the end of the ceremony.

He was the most marvellous man she had ever known, cared for her with tenderness and love, and because she loved him in the same way, she cared for him too. They were going to be happy together, she was sure of it.

Her starry gaze was fixed firmly on James as she walked down the aisle on Simon's arm, clasping his hand as she reached his side, barely aware of the words the vicar was speaking over them. She only came to a jolting awareness as the man on the other side of her moved to give her away in response to the vicar's question. It wasn't Simon!

She turned to find herself looking into warm hazel eyes, the hair that was brightly red on Penelope Sutcliffe a deep auburn on her brother, Giles.

He clasped her hand, squeezing it reassuringly, warmly, and moved to the back of the church to sit beside Penelope Dalby, the dark-haired man sitting beside her that Aura didn't recognise, probably her husband. Seated with them was a silver-haired woman, as frail-looking woman probably in her seventies. Grandmother Sutcliffe . . .?

Aura turned sharply back to James, receiving an encouraging smile from him. He was right, they were her family, they had a right to be here!

It was a beautiful ceremony, their vows spoken clearly and with love, gazing into each other's eyes, Aura vaguely aware of the fact that her mother was softly crying as she sat beside Helen.

She walked out of the church at James's side filled with pride, paling as they were met with a barrage of clicking cameras and reporters hurling questions at them!

'You're clearly over the death of your lover now, Miss Jones.'

'How long have you known each other?'

'Did you know your wife was once the mistress of Nigel Sutcliffe?'

Aura shut her ears to them after that last question, although she could feel James's tension beside her, knowing he wished for nothing more than to punch the foul-mouthed reporters in the face. And that he would do no such thing, for her sake. Selina had done this, she knew it!

'Did you know that your wife was regularly visited at her home by Mr Sutcliffe?' the pushy female reporter who had first questioned her persisted.

'And why shouldn't a father visit his daughter?'

Aura turned disbelievingly, to find not the Sutcliffes, or Helen, or Simon had come to her defence, but her *mother*!

'Meg——'

'I'm all right, James,' she assured him in a voice that, if it wasn't completely in control, was at least commanding. She turned to the dumb-struck reporters. 'Yes, you heard me correctly,' she told them contemptuously. 'Now if you don't mind, my daughter would like to get on with her wedding!'

'But who——?'

'What——?'

'Where——?'

'You heard the lady.' Giles Sutcliffe stepped forward to take Aura's mother's arm in a firm grip. 'Now get the hell out of here!'

'But aren't you——'

'You're Giles *Sutcliffe*!' the female reporter announced triumphantly over her colleague.

'And you're intruding on a private *family* occasion,' he bit out frostily.

Aura watched in fascination as the Sutcliffes closed ranks about her mother, ushering them to their car, finding herself in James's car a few seconds later.

'James, did you—did you hear——'

'Yes,' he confirmed gently. 'I heard.'

'But——'

'Darling,' his hand rested on hers. 'I think your mother has finally accepted your father's death.'

She couldn't believe it. Oh, her mother had eagerly helped her with the wedding arrangements the last month, but she had done it all from the flat, had never once attempted to leave the confines of that world again. And now this!

The Jaguar and limousine arrived at the flat at the same time, Aura's mother still looking a little dazed at being taken over by the Sutcliffe family.

'Meg?' James went to her concernedly.

'I'm all right,' she assured him with a shaky smile, turning to Aura. 'Oh, darling, I'm so sorry for the pain your father and I caused you!' Tears flooded her eyes and rolled down her cheeks. 'I've been the worst of all, retreating from the world and letting you take all the painful accusations.'

'Neither of you should have had to suffer the way that you did,' Giles Sutcliffe cut in grimly. 'No one should have to suffer that way just because they love someone.'

'Could we leave Aura and her mother alone for a while?' James requested gruffly, feeling her tremble at his side.

'We'll go upstairs,' Aura's mother told them. 'Please stay and join in the celebration of my daughter's wedding,' she invited the Sutcliffes. 'If you would like to,' she added uncertainly.

'Thank you,' the elderly silver-haired lady spoke for the first time. 'We would be honoured.'

Aura watched as her mother blinked back the tears, feeling like crying herself. The Sutcliffes had every reason to hate her and her mother, and yet they didn't.

'I guessed who "Mrs Dalby" was the night she came here,' her mother revealed once they were upstairs in her bedroom. 'Nigel was always very proud of his children,' she said with a catch in her voice. 'He carried photographs of all of you in his wallet.'

'Mummy, are you—are you really all right?' Aura looked at her closely.

She gave a shaky smile. 'I'd been fighting today's jolt into reality for a long time,' she revealed huskily. 'It started the night Marmaduke was almost killed, and although I tried to hold on to my fantasy world it was slowly receding. Today, when Giles stood by your side, as your father should have done, I knew I couldn't fight reality any more.' She clasped Aura's hands. 'Darling, I'm so sorry I let you face all that unpleasantness alone. Your father and I never meant to cause you pain because we loved each other.'

Aura hugged her. 'As long as I have you back again, none of it matters!'

Her mother gave a sad smile. 'Today I realised that Nigel is gone, that I have to go on without him, that

I'm your mother and it's time I started acting like it.'

'And the Sutcliffes?'

'They're your family, darling,' she said quietly. 'They very much want to acknowledge that. Giles told me his mother is dead now, that there's no one else to be hurt. They—they were very kind to me just now, but the final choice must lie with you.'

'I'd like to get to know them, but you and James are my family now.' Aura looked uncertain.

This time her mother's smile was encouraging. 'We humans have a great capacity for love; I'm sure you'll find room to love the Sutcliffes too!'

'Didn't she behave beautifully?' Aura smiled up at James.

'Of course,' he drawled. 'She's just like her mother.'

The two of them gazed down in rapt enjoyment of the tiny little girl who lay sleeping peacefully in her crib, completely unconcerned with the fact that as this was her christening day she was the centre of attention, all of her guests down in the lounge.

The last year had been the happiest Aura had ever known, she and James so much in love that it seemed their daughter's arrival couldn't possibly deepen that love, and yet it had. Neither of them could stop looking at the blonde-haired angel who had entered their life three months ago, completely captivating everyone she came into contact with. Her grandmother believed she was the most beautiful baby in the world, her Aunt Penelope and Uncle David often brought her cousin Rebecca over so that the two babies could coo at each other, and Uncle Giles spoilt his two nieces dreadfully. Grandmother Sutcliffe smiled down on all of them with perfect acceptance of the fact that her two great-granddaughters were stunning beauties.

'Do you think her mother and father could sneak away to be alone for an hour or so at her christening?' Aura suggested throatily.

James gave her a teasing look. 'Oh, I think it could be arranged.'

'When?'

'Now!'

Now Aura knew the answer to that question she had once asked herself; it was *wonderful* having a man like James come home to her every night, to share her life with him, to love with him.

With James at her side the future held only brightness and love, and both of them hoped that Stephanie would be only the first of their children. James deserved a big family to love and care for, and with nothing to mar their future Aura was perfectly happy to provide him with that family.

Maybe Stephanie's brother would be conceived this afternoon . . .!

# Take 4 best-selling love stories FREE
## Plus get a FREE surprise gift!

# PAMELA BROWNING

...is fireworks on the green at the Fourth of July and prayers said around the Thanksgiving table. It is the dream of freedom realized in thousands of small towns across this great nation.

But mostly, the Heartland is its people. People who care about and help one another. People who cherish traditional values and give to their children the greatest gift, the gift of love.

American Romance presents HEARTLAND, an emotional trilogy about people whose memories, hopes and dreams are bound up in the acres they farm.

HEARTLAND... the story of America.

Don't miss these heartfelt stories: American Romance #237 SIMPLE GIFTS (March), #241 FLY AWAY (April), and #245 HARVEST HOME (May).

HRT-1

# Harlequin Intrigue

Two exciting new stories each month.

Each title mixes a contemporary, sophisticated romance with the surprising twists and turns of a puzzler...romance with "something more."

Because romance can be quite an adventure.

## Romance, Suspense and Adventure